". . . keeps you on the edge of your seat."
—Roundtable Reviews for Kids

". . . a compelling portrait of a girl owning her
own strength and courage."
—Washington Parent

"Scenes depicting Lucy's resourcefulness are riveting."
—Booklist

". . . places a reassuringly typical American teenager in an
intriguingly different setting."
—School Library Journal

". . . works to bridge the gap between nationalities
and point out that people of all cultures have the
same goals, hopes, fears, and dreams."
—TeensReadToo.com

". . . an engrossing journey."
—Kirkus Reviews

". . . perfect for those African curriculum units and as a
suspenseful classroom read-aloud. . . . Stock up with multiple
copies—you won't be able to keep this one on the shelf!"
—Bookends: A Booklist Blog

"This book is impossible to put down."
—Kiwi magazine

For Nick, Joe, and Maya

First Chronicle Books LLC paperback edition published in 2011.

Text © 2009 by Eve Yohalem.
The Library of Congress has cataloged the original edition as follows:
Yohalem, Eve.
Escape under the forever sky / by Eve Yohalem.
p. cm.
Summary: As a future conservation zoologist whose mother is the United States Ambassador to Ethiopia, thirteen-year-old Lucy uses her knowledge for survival when she is kidnapped and escapes.
ISBN 978-0-8118-6653-8
[1. Survival–Fiction. 2. Kidnapping–Fiction
3. Mothers and daughters–Fiction. 4. Ethiopia–Fiction.] Title.
PZ7.Y7585Es 2009
[Fic]–dc22
2008019565

Book design by Alicia Mikles.
Typeset in Mrs. Eaves.
Cover photograph © Laura Flippen.

ISBN 978-0-8118-7874-6

Manufactured by C & C Offset, Longgang, Shenzhen, China, in September 2011.

3 5 7 9 10 8 6 4

This product conforms to CPSIA 2008.

Chronicle Books LLC
680 Second Street, San Francisco, California 94107

www.chroniclekids.com

ESCAPE UNDER THE FOREVER SKY

a novel by

Eve Yohalem

chronicle books · san francisco

Simien Mountains, Ethiopia

Dust is everywhere. Red-brown, soft as silt. It coats the windshield, the dashboard, our clothes, our skin. Streams of sweat trace tiny paths down my neck and bigger ones down my back. My legs stick to the seat.

The windows of the jeep are open. They let in a hot breeze that whips my hair but does nothing to cool us. They also let in more dust, which crusts inside our noses and throats.

But the open windows let us see out, let us see the sky. Huge forever sky, framed by mountain crags and undisturbed except by the eagles.

Below, farmers and their mud huts dot moorlands of dry, rocky earth. Bony cattle and goats graze among stands of giant lobelia trees.

"Stop!" I yell to Dahnie.

He slams on the breaks. "What is it, Lucy?"

"That *grass*," I whisper.

He raises an eyebrow at me.

"I've never seen anything like it," I explain.

Dahnie shrugs, happy to go along. He's used to me by now, the wildlife-obsessed American kid tagging along with the Ethiopian park ranger every chance she gets. I open the door and jump down onto the uneven dirt road. Dahnie gets out too. I notice that he leaves his rifle in the car. We're not going far.

Mounds of fluffy yellow grass pillow the hills on either side of the road, like something out of a Dr. Seuss book. I fight the urge to roll in its springy softness. Instead, I grab fistfuls and plunge my arms in halfway to my elbows, as deep as they will go.

Suddenly I hear thunder, even though the sky is a cloudless blue. I snatch back my arms and turn to Dahnie.

"What is it?" I ask him, anxious.

He backs slowly toward the car and motions for me to follow.

Masses of dark bodies crest the hilltop, taking on shape as they speed toward us. I'm frozen where I stand, my heartbeat nearly drowning out the roar, until Dahnie throws back his head and laughs.

It's hard to hear his voice over the avalanche. "Gelada baboons!" he yells.

Hundreds of huge monkeys pound the earth, shrieking at each other, ignoring us completely. They cross the road right in front of us.

"Go to them," Dahnie murmurs in my ear.

"What?" I spin around to look at him. "Are you crazy?"

"No, I am not. The geladas are the only species of baboon that is friendly to humans. They are vegetarian and perfectly safe. And this is the only place in the world where you will find them. Go!"

I take a slow step toward the ones that are crossing the road. Countless more continue to flood the hill above us.

"How many do you think there are?" I shout without taking my eyes off the stampeding horde.

"It is an entire troop. At least three hundred," he shouts back.

As soon as they cross the road, the baboons settle in the grass on the other side, all signs of wild frenzy gone. Some of them groom each other; some dig in the dirt looking for food. The males are massive, maybe fifty pounds each, brown as earth, with huge tufts of fur around their heads like lion manes and bright red triangles on their chests. They have long hourglass-shaped muzzles with deep wrinkles across the bridge, and their expressions seem to be saying to me, "How odd you are, O skinny furless one. But do walk among us if you must."

I'm maybe ten feet away now. I take another step. How close will they let me get? Closer, closer. Close enough to touch them now. I reach out my hand to a female, palm up. She looks at it and extends her own hand, which looks so much like mine. Closer—*no!*

I'm awake.

Chapter One

Day One

I was awake and in Ethiopia, but not in the Simien Mountains. In fact, I'd never been to the Simien Mountains, and at this rate I'd never go. Instead, I was in Addis Ababa, in my own house, in my own bed, living a life about as far from the adventure of my dream as it could possibly get.

We had moved here six months ago, when my mother became the American ambassador to Ethiopia. At around the same time, my father was offered a job in Indonesia with the World Bank, and my parents decided they could make the whole long-distance-family thing work. It didn't. My dad was supposed to come here once a month and every holiday, but it ended up being more like just Thanksgiving and Christmas. Meanwhile, my mother was working all the time, and I wasn't allowed out of the house except to go to school. That was mostly because of my mother's overprotectiveness and partly because of my own stupidity. But I'll get to my stupidity later.

This morning was typical of my nonexistence. After I woke up, I raced to check my e-mail. It was spring break, so my life was even more boring than usual. The only computer in the residence (that's what an ambassador's house is called—a residence) is downstairs in my mother's study. And because of all our heavy security, it's *slowww*. No IMing for me.

Thank God! There was an e-mail from Tana, which she'd sent last night after she'd gotten back from her family vacation in Spain. Tana's Ethiopian, and she's one of the two close friends I've managed to make here so far. Unfortunately, Americans aren't very popular at my school. The European kids seem to think that somehow it's our fault every time our government does something they hate. Tana and I go to the International School, which is where most of the ex-pat (as in *expatriate,* as in people who aren't Ethiopian but are living in Ethiopia, as in me) and rich Ethiopian kids go. Plus the usual handful of scholarship kids, like my other friend, Teddy, who was home visiting his family down south in Guge for the whole break.

Tana is everything I'm not: calm, patient, beautiful, charming. She's at least five inches taller than I am, with perfect posture and skin like melted milk chocolate (in contrast to my general gawkiness and freckles). My mother loves her. I would hate her except I know that all that loveliness is just a façade camouflaging a really brave and interesting person.

To: lucy

From: tana

Subject: everything

hi. i finally got your e-mail. ughhh. sounds UNBEARABLE. will your mother let u go on game drives again soon???? . . . it rained yesterday on our last day in paradise, so i told emama i had a headache and snuck down 2 the bar with a boy (!!!) while she,

ababa and tamirat went shopping. nothing
interesting to report . . . he was GERMAN
;-) . . . so happy 2 b home . . . can u come
over tomorrow?
xoxoxoxoxo . . . t
ps no matter how bored u r NO making crank
calls 2 SW . . . at least not without me!!!

I sighed. SW—Stephen Willet—is the best-looking boy in tenth grade—and a huge jerk. I see him sometimes at diplomatic shindigs because his father is the British ambassador. But even though we're usually the only people under fifty at these things, he somehow fails to notice that I exist.

To: tana
From: lucy
Subject: nothing
heyyy . . . i may b bored 2 death, but i'm not
that desperate!!! well, at least not for another
3 or 4 days. lol . . . game drives definitely not
happening anytime soon . . . we had another
HUGE fight about it last night. I'm starting 2
think she LIKES keeping me grounded at home

all the time. 1 less thing 4 her 2 have 2 think
about . . . I'll come over at 2. btw, there's
music today at mmmm my flavor. any
chance we can go?????
cul8r . . . me
ps u sure there's nothing INTERESTING to
report???

Mmmm My Flavor is a restaurant, and yes, that's really its name. Tana and I had been there a couple of times to hear some local bands, but there was no way my mother would let us go now. Ever since the Market Incident (*see* Lucy Hoffman's Stupidity), I'd been under total lockdown. I'd only just earned back Tana-visiting privileges. But I was hoping that maybe we'd get lucky and Tana's mom wouldn't be home, so we could sneak out.

With the highlight of my morning over, five empty hours stretched out ahead of me. I put in my contacts and took a quick shower, being careful to keep my mouth closed so I wouldn't swallow any of the microscopic parasites that lurk in the tap water. Then I twisted my wet hair into a ponytail, threw on some clothes, and headed outside to the veranda.

The veranda is my favorite place in the residence. It's basically just a big back patio covered by a sunshade. It has fans to keep the air moving and an incredibly comfy couch with soft green pillows that's a perfect place for reading. There's a table where I eat breakfast and lunch a lot of the time and where Iskinder and I build our card houses. Iskinder works in the residence, and I spend more time with him than with any other person here. I guess you could say he's the third close friend I've managed to make in Ethiopia.

It was pretty warm outside, even though it was still morning, so I stopped in the kitchen and poured myself a huge glass of iced Wush Wush tea, one of the local brands. Breakfast, as every healthy young woman knows, is the most important meal of the day, so I stuffed an entire chocolate-chip mini-muffin into my mouth. Then I grabbed a handful of granola from the plastic container on the counter and picked up the iced tea with my free hand.

After setting my glass on the table, I jogged to the middle of the back lawn to start my morning ritual. Standing perfectly still on the prickly dry grass, I whistled a long, fluttery call. I whistled again.

What an entrance: John, Paul, Ringo, and George—superb starlings I had befriended after two very patient weeks of making tempting overtures with wilted lettuce, dried mango, and other birdie delicacies. They swooped down and clustered two birds on each wrist, gently pecking my closed fists, where they knew I was hiding their breakfast. Their talons felt like pinpricks on my skin. I marveled at their glossy feathers, a psychedelic rainbow of iridescent blue, green, orange, and white.

"Morning, guys," I said softly, opening my fingers so they could enjoy their meal. "I brought your favorite today."

I've always been good with animals. They've been my passion for as long as I can remember. Back home in Bethesda, when I was little, I'd had absolutely no interest in dolls, but I had mountains of stuffed dogs, bears, lions, tigers, monkeys, even a wild boar named Schweinken. My mom offered to get me one of those amazing African grey parrots that live to be seventy years old and speak in full sentences, but I think it's wrong to keep animals in cages.

"Hi, Luce, what's on tap for today?" It was my

mother, and of course the instant the Fab Four heard her, they flew away. Annoyed, I turned around.

She looked impeccable, as always. Her gray pantsuit and white shirt would be as crisp and clean at the end of the day as they were now. She carried her briefcase in one hand and her silver coffee thermos in the other. Tall and perfectly proportioned, with my straw blonde hair and her own brown eyes, my mother looks like the kind of woman who should be riding horses in Virginia, not running an embassy in Africa.

"What's on tap? Let's see. First I thought I'd go play some tennis in the park, then maybe meet a bunch of friends for ice cream, and then go hang out at the mall."

She raised her right eyebrow at me, unamused but unwilling to take the bait.

"Tana's home. I'm going over there later."

"Okay. Iskinder will drive you. Ask him to wait at Tana's house until you're ready to go home."

Hmm. I see we're still having some trust issues. "Fine."

"Have fun, Lu. I'll be home late tonight."

What else is new?

By the way, my mother wasn't always as self-centered and no fun as she is now. Let's just say there's an inverse relationship between how much she cares about her job and how much she cares about me.

I lay down on my favorite couch and leaned over to look through the stack of books on the floor. There were a bunch about African wildlife, plus the usual autobiographies by my heroes: Jane Goodall, Dian Fossey, and Biruté Galdikas. They're the three women who were sponsored by the famous anthropologist Louis Leakey to study the great apes in the wild in a way that no one had ever done before. People call them Leakey's Angels. If everything goes according to plan, I'll be doing exactly what they do in ten or fifteen years. Which means I need to be prepared. I decided to reread *Haines's Guide to African Mammals*, fifth edition, for the umpteenth time.

Around one o'clock, Iskinder came out with a tray of what he calls toasted cheese. It's my favorite lunch, so he makes it for me almost every day. Iskinder's toasted cheese is like regular grilled cheese except he leaves off the top, puts on a slice of tomato, and adds some secret ingredient that makes the whole thing superdelicious. I keep asking him what the secret is, but he won't tell me. He just puts on his wise-old-man expression, the one that says, *Ah, Lucy, life is richer with a little mystery.*

He set the tray on the table. "Come. It is time you eat lunch now, Lucy."

Iskinder is a small, thin man with snow-white hair, a high forehead, and skin the color of well-done toast. His eyes stick out a little, and they look even bigger behind his round wire-rimmed glasses. He reminds me of Owl in *Winnie-the-Pooh.*

"Thanks," I said. I brought over my Wush Wush, sat down, and began to inhale the sandwiches while Iskinder watched me, highly amused.

"I cannot understand how all those sandwiches fit inside someone so small," he said. I knew Iskinder was just trying to be funny, but I couldn't help taking it personally. I *am* really small, and it's kind of a sore spot. I'm thirteen and not even five feet tall yet. My father says I shouldn't worry, because everyone in his family was a late bloomer, and he was really short until high school. I hope I don't have to wait that long. It's mortifying to look like everybody's little sister.

"Okay, so give me the Araya update," I said. The Arayas are Iskinder's next-door neighbors, and their lives are like something straight out of a soap opera.

"Oh, there is big news today, Lucy. Very big news. Kaleb is coming home in three weeks, and you should see Mrs. Araya and Lishan running around the house getting everything ready."

"Kaleb? Isn't he the one who's been living in America? The one who broke off his engagement to that girl everyone thought he shouldn't marry anyway?"

"The very same. And she has a new boyfriend now, so it will be interesting to see what happens when Kaleb comes home."

"*Very* interesting," I agreed. "Hey, do you know what today is?" I asked.

"Tuesday?"

"Well, yeah, but it's also the first day I'm allowed to go out!"

"The green couch will look very empty without you lying on it all day long."

I rolled my eyes at him. "Very funny, Iskinder. Do you mind taking me to Tana's when I'm done with lunch?"

He smiled at me. "No problem, Lucy. No problem at all." The way Iskinder pronounces it, you can hear the *t* in *at*.

I munched in silence for a couple of minutes. "How about some urban development after dinner tonight?" I asked. This is our inside joke. Iskinder and I build card houses together. But not just regular card houses. We build whole cities of them, all different shapes and sizes, and pretend they're places like an Italian piazza, an American town, or an Ethiopian village. Iskinder is amazing at building card houses. He can build them six stories high, or round, or even pyramid shaped. He's taught me everything I know, and I have to say, I'm pretty good now. Of course, that says as much about how much time I've spent stuck in the house over the last six months as it does about my building skills.

"I look forward to it," he said, smiling.

I finished eating, and we agreed to meet in front of the house in fifteen minutes. I checked my watch. It has a little compass on it, which told me I was facing northeast, plus two time zones, which said it was 5:03 in the morning back home in Maryland and 1:03 in the afternoon here. But no matter how I measure time, I always have way too much of it to kill.

Chapter Two

Iskinder was waiting when I got outside, holding open the back door of the BPM, a.k.a. our bulletproof Mercedes. I buckled up and slumped back with my feet propped up on the passenger seat in front of me.

"Syed Ibrahim Kausri, the infamous Pakistani drug baron, is being held here in Addis Ababa while he awaits extradition to the United States, where he faces charges of conspiracy to import, manufacture, and distribute heroin." The local news blared from the car radio until Iskinder changed the station. Then we began the drive through the pocket of alien suburbia that is the American embassy compound.

Most of the Americans who work at the embassy live here, inside the compound. There are nine other houses, but our residence is the biggest. When you add in the administration buildings, the whole spread is pretty impressive. It's like living in a kind of weird pseudo-neighborhood, with little kids and dogs and gardeners mowing lawns. The compound is surrounded by tall flowering trees and bushes. We need all that greenery so we can pretend not to notice the massive cement wall, topped by a foot of razor wire, that separates us from the outside world.

As we drove through the front gate, I mock-saluted Henry, the marine at the security station. Once we were outside the compound, we were no longer under constant observation by U.S. military forces, but that didn't mean I had any more freedom. I stared out the window at Addis Ababa, the capital of one of the world's oldest civilizations, and I thought about how the inside of a car is as close as I ever get to the city.

Everything looks so different from back home. I watched boys leading donkeys loaded with firewood along the side of the road, goats running wild, and women wrapped in white *shema* shawls reaching up with one hand to steady the bundles of firewood on their heads. Japanese cars zipped in and out of traffic lanes along with blue and white taxis. There were also minibus taxis, the ones that people call cars of conversation because so many people are crammed inside that you can't help but chat with your neighbors (not that I would know since I've never been allowed in one). Barbershops, jewelry stores, and small groceries were mixed in with rows of corrugated-tin strip malls spilling out fabric, batteries, and bananas.

It didn't take long to get to Tana's. Like a lot of other rich Ethiopians, she and her family live in a big house surrounded by a high stone wall. Iskinder checked in through the intercom at the gate, and we pulled into the driveway. When we got to the front of the house, I said oh-so-casually, "Thanks, Iskinder. I'll call you when I'm ready to go home. Probably around five."

Iskinder turned around in his seat to look at me. "That is all right, Lucy. I will wait for you."

"Don't worry, Iskinder. I'll be fine. You can just come back at five."

"I am sorry, Lucy, but your mother asked me to stay here with you until it is time to leave."

Not just trust issues. *Big* trust issues.

"Please, Iskinder?" I pleaded in my most winsome voice, oozing charm with a hint of pathetic. "It would mean so much to me. It's my first time with Tana since everything happened—you know that. I *promise* I won't do anything I shouldn't do."

Iskinder hesitated. I could see him debating with himself.

"*Please?*" Big eyes, small smile . . .

It worked.

"Ah, Lucy, how can I say no to you?"

"Thanks, Iskinder!"

Ignoring the hard lump of guilt I already felt in the pit of my stomach, I gave Iskinder a hug and headed up the path leading to the house, passing the Kassais' new driver on the way. He stared at me as I walked by him, and I noticed the two lines of skin that bisected his left eyebrow, scars called "elevens" because they look like that number. A lot of people have them here. When children are born, parents cut their eyebrows because they believe the blood will prevent eye disease.

Tana swung the door open before I even had a chance to ring the bell.

"Lucy!"

Instantly I forgot all about Iskinder and my mother. I was just so happy to finally be out of the house and with my friend. We hugged each other, and then Tana hooked her arm through mine, grinning. "I have good news," she whispered. "My mother is going shopping in a few minutes with her friend Mrs. Beshir. So we can find something to do *outside*." I got the hint. *Like go to Mmmm My Flavor.*

I thought about my promise to Iskinder. *Technically,* I wasn't breaking it, since I didn't believe that going to hear some music with my friend was something I shouldn't do.

I grinned back. "Fantastic!" Then I noticed the new driver watching us. Tana and I walked into the house together, and I asked, "What's with Mr. Happy out there?"

"Who, Dawit?" she asked.

I nodded.

"Nothing. He is our new driver. My dad loves him—he never speaks, and he is never late."

"He gives me the creeps," I said.

"Don't worry. We will not be here to see him, right?"

Before I could answer, Tana's mother came bustling into the front hall. "Lucy! I thought I heard your voice."

I put my hands together and bowed slightly. "Salaam, Weizero Nadia." *Weizero* means "Mrs.," and Nadia is Mrs. Kassai's first name.

We kissed each other four times, left cheek–right cheek, left cheek–right cheek. "Very good, Lucy," she said. "You sound just like a proper Ethiopian girl."

"Amasegenallo." That means "thank you" in Amharic, the language most people speak in this part of the country.

"And how is your mother? Is she well?"

"Yes, thank you, Mrs. Kassai. She's very well."

"I am happy to hear it. And your father?"

"He's very well too, thank you."

"And what about your animals? Have you been out in the bush recently?"

Ouch. "No, not recently. But very soon, I hope."

Mrs. Kassai beamed at me and then leaned forward for another hug and two kisses. Ethiopian greetings can go on for half an hour. If we didn't do something soon, Mrs. Kassai would start asking after my goldfish back home in Bethesda. I gave Tana a pleading look, and she came to the rescue.

"Emama, Mrs. Beshir will be here soon, yes?"

Mrs. Kassai looked at her watch. "*Ow*, Tana. Yes, any minute. Okay, my girls, have fun today. Makda is here if you need anything." A car honked outside. "*Ishi, ishi!*" she called—okay, okay. "Ciao," she said to us, with two more kisses each. *Ciao* is a leftover from when the Italians occupied Ethiopia during World War II.

"Ciao, Mrs. Kassai."

"Ciao, Emama."

We waved at Mrs. Kassai from the doorway.

"Ten, nine, eight," Tana counted down out of the side of her mouth until the coast was clear.

"Makda's upstairs?" I whispered.

Tana nodded and kept counting. "Seven, six, five—"

I couldn't wait any more. "One!"

Chapter Three

Tana and I held hands as we walked toward the restaurant. Friends do that here—boys and boys, girls and girls, even men and other men. What you never see is men and women holding hands. That would be considered way too risqué.

Zewditu Street was quiet in the early afternoon. Jacaranda trees lined the center island of the road, their flowers bursting from the branches like clusters of lavender grapes. I inhaled, but I couldn't tell if they had any fragrance because the air smelled like fire, like it always does in Africa. I used to love the tangy, smoky scent, but then I found out it comes from the firewood that everyone burns for fuel, which is part of the reason why there are practically no trees left in the country—a total ecological nightmare.

Half a block away from the restaurant we could already hear the music. It sounded like Western pop mixed with some Middle Eastern twang. Tana and I started singing along and shimmying our shoulders Ethiopian-style. We were so caught up in our own little world that we didn't notice the three boys following us until it was too late. They clustered around us in height order, Small, Medium, and Large.

"Hallo!" said Large.

"Hi!" said Small.

Medium just smiled, showing us teeth that were already looking brown with decay. In Ethiopia only the very rich can afford dentists.

"Hi," I answered, feeling the way I always do in this situation: kind of excited about meeting Ethiopian street kids, kind of nervous about being hit up for something.

Everywhere I go in Ethiopia—well, at least when I'm allowed out of the car—kids pop out of nowhere to bombard me with the same three questions: "You are from America?" "You want a . . . [*fill in blank:* necklace, fake antique coin, toothbrush stick, religious icon, etc.]?" and—my personal favorite—"Gimme pen?" There must be a line in all the tourist guidebooks under the heading "Social Graces" or maybe "Guilt" that says, "Travelers to Ethiopia should bring about five hundred ballpoint pens to give to local children, thereby encouraging them to beg without actually giving them any kind of meaningful help."

Luckily, I was with Tana, who got rid of them in about ten seconds.

"What did you say?" I asked.

She gave me one of her demure smile-behind-her-hand looks. "I told the big one I recognized him from his school and asked if he would like me to call his mother and tell her that he has been begging in the streets."

"You know his mother?"

"Of course not!"

This is why I love Tana.

The band was playing in the outdoor garden behind the restaurant. It wasn't too crowded, and the host gave us a table right in front of the platform that they were using as a stage. We had just gotten our

Pepsis and I was humming along in my tuneless way when Tana kicked my shin under the table.

"Ow!"

"Over there," she whispered. "Dawit!"

He was standing in the doorway, scanning the garden while the host pointed in our direction.

"Let's get out of here," I said, pushing back my chair to get up.

But it was too late. Dawit had already spotted us and was on his way over. Tana and I locked eyes. *We're in so much trouble.*

"Tana," Dawit said.

Tana stood up and put her hands on her hips. "What are you doing here, Dawit?" I could tell she was trying to sound authoritative.

"Your mother forgot her wallet. She came back for it, and when she saw you were gone, she asked me to bring you home."

We were doomed, and we knew it. Resigned to our fate, we followed Dawit to the car.

"Mrs. Kassai asked me to bring you home also, Lucy. I will drop off Tana first."

No way. My only hope was that I could go back to

Tana's house, wait for Iskinder to come for me at five o'clock, and pray Mrs. Kassai wouldn't tell my mother.

"Thanks, Dawit, but you don't have to take me home. Our driver is already coming for me."

"Mrs. Kassai said bring you home now."

Something in his voice told me the situation was hopeless.

Tana grabbed my hand and squeezed it. She knew that between this and what had happened at the market, my mother would probably send me to my room for the rest of my life and post a marine guard outside my door. Everyone's parents make these kinds of threats. The difference is my mother can actually follow through on them.

As we pulled into Tana's driveway, a thought occurred to me: How had Dawit known where to find us? But before I had a chance to ask Tana, she climbed out with one last sympathetic look.

"I will e-mail you," she said.

"Me too," I promised. I leaned back in my seat and closed my eyes. My pathetic life was about to get even worse.

After a couple of minutes I opened my eyes again

and looked out the window. The neighborhood didn't look familiar.

"Um, Dawit?" I said. "This isn't the way to my house. I live in the American embassy compound."

"It is a shorter way," he said. I could see the scars over his eye in the rearview mirror. "There is too much traffic in the middle of the city at this time of the day."

I pressed my eyelids down with my fingers, trying to stop the tears of self-pity that were threatening to spill out. *She's going to ground me until I go to college.*

I looked out the window again. We were definitely in a part of the city I had never seen before. My heart started pounding, and I sat up straighter, trying to get a better view out the front.

"Dawit?"

He didn't answer. My whole body went numb.

"Stop the car *now*, Dawit."

Nothing. We sped past a cluster of shanty houses and a few random shopping stalls, clearly not headed anywhere near the American embassy. I looked frantically for a traffic light where he would have to stop, but there weren't any.

"Look, Dawit, you don't know who you're dealing with! My mother is the United States ambassador, and you're going to be in big trouble. Stop the car *now*!"

Suddenly Dawit swerved to the side of the road and braked so fast the tires squealed. I flung open the car door, but I couldn't get out. A man I had never seen before was blocking my way. He shoved me back inside and started to climb in after me.

"Get away from me!" I screamed.

I lunged for the other door, but the man grabbed my leg and yanked me back. Clutching a fistful of my hair with one hand, he stuffed a dirty rag into my face with the other. I couldn't scream anymore, but I kicked and twisted as hard as I could until he jammed his knee into my hip. All I could see of him were his crooked brown teeth. Gasping for breath, I kept struggling even as I felt myself slipping away, out of my body, out of the car, into the air.

Chapter Four

Night One

It hurts. Everything hurts so bad. It's so hot I can't breathe. There's a stink like sour milk. And I can't . . . I can't see. . . . Why can't I see? Oh God, oh God, oh God, oh God, oh God. I have to SEE!

It's a blindfold.

No! Get it off! Get it off!! GET. IT. OFF!!!

But I can't move my arms. WHERE ARE MY HANDS???

My hands were tied behind my back, so numb I could hardly feel them. Furiously, I rubbed my face against the scratchy pad I was lying on, trying to inch off the blindfold. My right cheek was scraped raw before I finally worked it off.

What I saw in the dim light was petrifying: *I am nowhere.*

Nowhere was a small room. A dirt floor, tin roof, scrap-wood shack with a mat, a crate, a kerosene lamp. And me.

Lying awkwardly on my side with my arms pinned behind my back, I gazed up at the ceiling, tears streaming from the corners of my eyes. The salt water stung my cheek, but I couldn't wipe it away. I lay like that for a really long time. *Where am I? What's happening? Mom, Mom, Mom . . .*

I saw that one of the wallboards was too short, leaving a small opening near the ceiling. There was no screen over it, which meant that a lot of nasty beasts could get in: mosquitoes carrying malaria, rabid bats, giant stinging beetles that could fly into my hair and pierce my scalp with their huge, snapping pincers, venomous snakes, poisonous lizards.

That's why all the windows at the residence have screens. Oh God, I want to go home.

What am I going to do? How am I supposed to know what to do?

Maybe . . . maybe I could start by sitting up.

No. No way. Not yet.

I lay very still and quiet, trying to calm down so I could think clearly. I took big, deep breaths until finally my chest didn't shudder anymore when I exhaled.

Okay. Now.

First I had to get my hands in front of my body. I rolled onto my back and, grateful for my six years of gymnastics, folded myself into an upside-down pike position, with my legs and feet pointed straight back behind my head so my knees touched my nose. Then I wiggled my bound hands out from under my back, bent my knees to my chin and pushed my feet through the circle of my arms. My shoulders burned with that excruciating prickly ache you get from being stuck in a bad position for too long. I stared at the rope that bound my wrists. It was thick and a little frayed, and the knot looked complicated. I tried to pull my wrists apart, but there was no give at all. This thing wasn't coming off without a knife. My stomach lurched.

Okay, now I'll sit up. Here we go, Lucy, on three.

One. Two. Three.

I sat up slowly because moving hurt so much. It felt like there were a hundred ice picks stabbing my head. Plus, my contact lenses were glued to my eyeballs, and my ribs and right hip were throbbing. What was wrong with my hip? I lifted up my T-shirt. There wasn't much light, but I could see a huge bruise, purple and swollen. It must have happened when the man with the nasty teeth jammed me with his knee.

I could still feel that dirty rag smothering my face. It was hard to breathe again. I yanked up my knees and buried my eyes in my kneecaps, hugging my legs as hard as I could. *Mom, where are you? Please, please, please, come get me. Daddy, help me, please . . .*

I cried and cried until my sobs squeezed out some of my fear, leaving behind a numb, empty void. *Let me just curl up into a ball and die.*

Okay, Lucy, somehow you're going to deal with this. Three deep breaths and then you'll figure out what to do next.

One. Two. Three.

I tried to focus on what a scientist would do in a dangerous, unfamiliar situation. What would Jane, Dian, and Biruté do? *Hey, Dian Fossey was kidnapped too, and she survived.* I refused to think about the fact that a few years later she was murdered. *Completely different circumstances, totally unrelated.*

I'm sure every police officer in Ethiopia is looking for me right now. They're probably almost here already. I bet my mother called the president of the United States, who called the prime minister of

Ethiopia and told him to find me or else. My parents will do whatever they have to do to get me back. They will pay any ransom, gather an army, and never stop until they find me.

But what could I do in the meantime? What did Leakey's Angels do when they first got to the bush, deep in the heart of nowhere? They made hypotheses. They observed. They considered the facts.

Then they took action.

I crisscrossed my legs and exhaled. First, I'd note my surroundings: I was sitting on a straw mat that was covered by a brown wool blanket. The room had one small opening near the ceiling and one door. There was one wooden crate with one kerosene lamp on top of it. Since the lamp made the only light in the room, it had to be nighttime. I checked my watch: 10:13 pm. And fourteen seconds, fifteen seconds, sixteen seconds, seventeen seconds. *Stop.* The kerosene lamp probably also meant there was no electricity here, wherever here was. It was hot even though it was night, so here was probably somewhere at a lower altitude than Addis. *Great, that narrows it down to about fifty percent of the country.*

The only other thing in the room was a bucket.

Next, I observed myself. I was wearing a black T-shirt and green cotton pants, underwear, a hair elastic, and my watch, with its two time zones and compass. My sandals were gone. I was sweating, and my ribs and my right hip hurt. My contact lenses felt like sandpaper, but I couldn't take them out because I'd be completely blind without them.

I have to pee.

Oh no, I seriously have to pee. What am I going to do? No way, not the bucket. Ugh. I can't believe I have to pee in that bucket. There's no toilet paper either.

It's amazing what you can do with your hands tied together if you're lucky enough to be wearing pants with an elastic waistband. One small victory for Lucy.

What's going on? Why did they kidnap me? Who are they? I thought maybe it was because of Mom's job. Or maybe it was just about ransom. The kidnappers might have thought my family was really rich because we're American, even though we're not because both my parents have government jobs. But I guess compared with most Ethiopians, we are rich. *Who knows?*

I should have known better. After my giant stupidity at the market, I should have known better.

Chapter Five

It was my idea to cut last-period study hall—I couldn't stand the agony of waiting one second more. Racing the two blocks from school, Tana, Teddy, and I just managed to catch the bus before it pulled away from the stop. It was painted the usual ketchup red and mustard yellow with the lion of Judah, the national symbol of Ethiopia, emblazoned on the side, rearing on its hind legs and pawing the air. I was so excited I practically high-fived it. This was my first time on any kind of Ethiopian public transportation.

We gave the driver the two-birr fare (about twenty-five cents) and smushed our way through the packed aisle to crowd around a pole halfway back. We were in our school uniforms, but somehow Tana looked like the next teen movie queen in her plaid jumper while I looked like Raggedy Ann in mine. And Teddy—well, with his long eyelashes and the way his smile flashes against his dark skin, he looks hot no matter what he wears. But I knew that thinking of Teddy that way was bad for our friendship, so I tried to stop myself whenever it happened (which I had to admit was a lot).

"What did you tell your mother?" Tana asked me.

"That I was going to your house after school," I said. "What about you?"

"That I was going to your house." She smiled.

"I told the matron I was going to the *mercato*." Teddy boards at school, since his home is in Guge, a small village near the lake region in the south.

"You told her the truth?"

"Why not? She asked me to bring her some prayer candles."

I rolled my eyes. "How come boys here get to do whatever they want, and girls can't do anything? I bet you can stay out all night in your village and no one cares."

"I guess so," he said, his shoulders tensing. He looked away from us out the window.

It's hard to get Teddy to talk about his village. Partly because he doesn't feel the need to share every detail of his life the way I do, but also because it's painful for him. Both of Teddy's brothers had died. He hasn't told us why, but it's not hard to guess—half a million Ethiopian kids die every year from disease and bad nutrition, and it's even worse for the poorest families, like Teddy's. Before he came to Addis, Teddy had to walk six kilometers to the next village to go to school—and he felt lucky, because most of his friends didn't go to school at all. But a better education wasn't the only reason his parents were so desperate for Teddy to get his scholarship. They wanted him to be someplace where he could get good medical care and enough food to eat, so they wouldn't lose the only son they had left.

So all we know about Teddy's village is that there are *tukuls* (the mud huts people live in), a few shops, the church, and an Internet café. Oh, and a foosball table. Right in the middle of the street.

I felt bad about bringing up the subject of home. I

started to apologize, but Tana interrupted me.

"Lucy, if you think it is bad to be a girl here, just imagine what it is like to be a woman. Men are in charge of everything! It is that way with my parents, with their friends, with everyone I know. And it never changes. When I grow up, they will all expect me to behave a certain way just because that is how it has always been. I *hate* it."

I was shocked. Cool, controlled Tana was really worked up.

"Is it because your family's Muslim?" I asked her.

"What she says is true for everyone," Teddy said. "It is the same in my village, and we are all Christians."

Tana took a deep breath. "That is why next year I am going to ask my parents to send me to high school in London, with my cousins who live there."

"Tana! You can't leave!"

Before Tana could answer, the driver made an announcement over the loudspeaker in Amharic. Then he repeated it in English: "Attention, passengers. There are many pickpockets riding the buses in Addis Ababa. Please protect your belongings."

My hands shot to the front pocket of my messenger bag, which was slung across my right shoulder. Tana and Teddy laughed.

"Ferenji!" they said at the same time. *Ferenji* means "foreigner."

"What do you mean?"

"You just showed the pickpockets exactly where you keep your wallet," Teddy said.

"Okay, I officially feel stupid," I said.

Just then the bus stopped at the market, and Teddy put his arm around me, guiding me toward the door.

"Don't worry," he said. "We will not let anything bad happen to the ambassador's daughter. After all, we do not want to start an international incident."

I didn't respond. I was too busy concentrating on keeping my face normal and trying to ignore the tiny electric shocks that started racing through my body the second he touched me.

They say the *mercato* in Addis Ababa is the largest outdoor market in Africa. I don't know if that's true, but it's pretty huge. Nothing I had heard, none of the pictures I had seen, prepared me for the real thing. People competed with cars, trucks, and donkeys for space on the packed streets. Endless alleyways were crammed with stalls offering everything under the sun: hubcaps, firewood, luggage, fabric, flower-print mattresses, stuffed animals, shoes, backpacks, plastic water jugs, nail polish, and tons of electronics. Weirdest of all were the rows of white plastic mannequins with rainbow-sherbet hair. I stopped to look at a display of brightly colored bundles of straw. "For weaving baskets," Tana explained.

Old women sat on orange blankets on the ground, selling the two-foot-long wicks used to make prayer candles. We passed a boy sewing "national clothes," the traditional toga-style wraps made from Ethiopian *shemas,* his needle moving so lightning fast that his hand was a blur. A flatbed truck passed us with a man perched on top of a huge covered load, an oil drum— *an oil drum*—balanced on his head. And the sound of the place! Afternoon prayers blared over loudspeakers from the Christian church nearby, not even coming close to drowning out the noise from the crowds of shoppers and merchants hawking their wares. Curry from the spice market flavored the air. I had never been so happy.

As we wandered around the stalls, I noticed there were no prices on anything.

"Is this one of those markets where you bargain for stuff?" I asked.

Teddy looked confused. "You have never been to a market before?"

I shook my head. "No, I have. I used to go with my father in Morocco. He let me try to buy things a couple of times, but I was pathetic at it," I admitted. "I always felt so weird about negotiating. I never knew what to say."

Teddy and Tana exchanged a look, surprised, I think, that something that came so naturally to them was so foreign to me. I guess it would be as if they'd come to America and I'd found out they didn't know how to use a credit card.

"Bargaining is like a game," Teddy explained. "It is not so difficult if you understand the rules and much more fun than your way of shopping."

"We will show you," Tana said. "Tewodros," she ordered, using Teddy's full name, "go and buy me a basket, please."

Tana handed Teddy some money and waved her

hand in the direction of the basket stalls. "We will let the boy do the work," she whispered to me. "They will give him a better price."

"As you wish, Weizero Tana," Teddy joked, adding a respectful bow.

"And make sure it is an old one!" Tana called after him. "They are much better quality than the new ones," she explained.

"How can you tell if they're old?" I asked.

"The colors are not so bright, and the stitches are smaller and more even. Shhh. Watch Teddy now."

There was a row of identical basket stalls, and Teddy casually approached the first one. It was tiny, the walls and floor stuffed with stacks of colorful baskets of every variety, from huge platters with domed lids to small bowls and jewelry boxes.

Ignoring the proprietor, Teddy picked up a small basket. The proprietor said something to him in Amharic, and with a scornful shrug of his shoulders Teddy put the basket down and walked away without a word. He winked at us.

"What's going on?" I asked Tana.

"The man asked him for one hundred sixty birr.

 44

Teddy wants to show him that such a price is not even worth considering," she said as Teddy approached the next stall.

"Now he is telling the owner that the first man offered to sell him a basket for one hundred sixty birr, and he is asking if he can do better. Ah, you see, the owner says he will sell him the basket for one hundred twenty-five birr." Teddy walked away again, ignoring the owner, who followed him, calling, *"Ishi! Ishi!"* and some other stuff I didn't understand.

This went on several more times. I watched, fascinated, as the price dropped from stall to stall. Tana kept translating for me. "He says, 'This is not machine made. It is handmade. Look at the quality!' and 'Please, I have a family to feed. You know this is a very good price, the best I can do.'"

Finally Teddy returned, triumphant. "Sixty-five birr! And you can tell it is a real Harari basket." I was impressed. Teddy had bargained them down from twenty dollars to about eight.

Teddy started to unwrap the package to show us, but he was interrupted by shouts several stalls away.

"What's going on?" I asked, standing on my toes to

try to see over the crowd. People swarmed toward us, jostling us, clearly trying to get away from whatever was happening. Someone slammed into me, and I jerked back when he yanked hard on my messenger bag. Before I could grab it, the bag was gone and whoever had taken it had disappeared into the crowd.

"Hey!" I yelled.

But my mind must have been playing tricks on me because I thought I heard someone calling my name.

"Lucy, over there! They are calling you." Tana pointed straight ahead, and sure enough, there were half a dozen U.S. marines shouting, "Lucy Hoffman! Lucy Hoffman!"

Completely mortified, I looked at my friends' shocked faces. *My mother.*

Chapter Six

"What you did was incredibly dangerous! I don't know what you were thinking!" We were back at the residence, and I was awaiting sentencing.

"Everything would have been fine if you hadn't sent in the SWAT team!"

"Lucy—" my mother started, and then changed her mind. "Iskinder, help me out here."

Iskinder wore the concerned and serious expression of a mortician. "I would not let my own mother go to the *mercato* alone."

Traitor.

"There, do you understand now?"

"Yes, I understand! I understand that you never let

me do anything. Maybe if you let me actually go out once in a while, I wouldn't have to sneak around!"

"For God's sake, Lucy, someone cut the bag from your body. With a knife!"

"Which they never would have been able to do if I hadn't been so distracted by the marines. It's *your* fault I lost my bag!"

"Really?" Her voice was calm and quiet all of a sudden. A bad sign. "Well, it's your fault you won't be leaving this house except to go to school for the next month. You think you're so responsible? Then you can take responsibility for lying and for putting yourself and your friends in a dangerous situation."

Grounded for an entire month? No game drives, no Tana or Teddy? *What am I going to do all day, every day, completely alone?*

"You don't care what you do to me. You don't care how I feel. You're cruel and selfish," I spat out at her. My words hit home. I saw the pain in my mother's eyes, and even though I was angry, I felt bad about hurting her. But I stalked past her and up the stairs to my bedroom anyway, slamming the door behind me.

• • •

It hurt to look back on what I'd done that day. Like I said, I should have known better. But I couldn't dwell on my regrets, because suddenly I heard men talking on the other side of the wall! My heart pounded so hard I thought my chest would burst. Their voices were low and intense. I sat up and pressed my ear against the rough wall so I could hear better. I guessed there were two of them, but it was hard to tell, especially since they weren't speaking English. It sounded like Amharic, but what do I know? It could have been any one of the seventy languages people speak in Ethiopia. But if they were speaking Amharic, it meant they were Ethiopian. Was it Dawit and Nasty Teeth, two new monsters, or (*please, please, please*) someone to rescue me? I couldn't tell. Hypothesis: I had been kidnapped by greater than or equal to two Ethiopian men. The door swung open, and I held my breath.

It was a woman. A white woman. *They're here!* Relief washed over me; I could hardly believe it. The whole horrible nightmare was over; my parents were on their way. I leaped off the mat. I wanted to hug her, but my wrists were still bound together. Plus, she was holding a plate in one hand and a pitcher in the other.

"How did you find me? Where's my mother? When can we go?" The questions came tumbling out—I was just so incredibly, ecstatically relieved.

"Find you?" Her accent sounded British.

"Yes, how did you know where I was? Do you know who did this? Where are they?"

"Sorry to disappoint, Lucy, but I didn't *find* you, I *brought* you."

I didn't get it. What was she saying? She couldn't mean . . . "Wha—why . . . ?" I stammered. "I don't understand."

"You are here because we brought you here. And if everyone cooperates and you behave yourself, you'll go home. That's all you need to understand."

My knees buckled, and I crashed back down onto the mat. I couldn't believe it. She was one of them. Just because she was white, I had assumed she was on my side. *Great, now I'm an idiot AND a racist.*

She was silent, letting the news sink in. I stared at the dirt floor so she wouldn't see me fighting back the tears.

"Stand up," she said at last.

I cringed, shrinking back to the corner of my mat.

She was holding a huge hunting knife with a thick blade at least six inches long.

"Give me your hands."

I couldn't move.

"Go on, give them to me. I see you've managed to take off the blindfold. Would you prefer to keep the rope?"

I held out my hands but kept my face turned away so I wouldn't have to watch her work that terrifying thing through the rope. When it finally came off, there were deep red welts on my skin. I massaged my wrists to get some of the circulation back.

"I brought you some food." She put the pitcher on the crate and handed me a plate of *injera*, a fermented Ethiopian bread. I couldn't even look at it; there was a baseball where my stomach should have been.

"Now listen to me carefully, Lucy, because if you follow the rules, you will be fine. And if you don't follow the rules, you will be dead."

That got my attention. My head snapped up to look at her pale, angular face. She was grown up but young. Not tall, not short. Her brown hair was in a neat ponytail, and she was wearing khaki pants and a white polo shirt. She looked like a tennis instructor with bad skin, which I realize is an oxymoron. *Who is this person, and why is she doing this to me?*

"You are going to be here for a few days, until your mother does what she needs to do. During that time you will stay in this room. You will be brought food and water. Don't bother yelling for help because there's no one around to hear you. Don't even think of trying to escape because if our dogs don't get you, the hyenas will. If you make any kind of trouble at all, we will hurt you. If you make trouble a second time, we will kill you." She paused. "Do you understand?"

I nodded.

"Good."

I heard her lock the door behind her.

I stuffed my shirt into my mouth so no one would hear me, and I cried for a long time, swallowing air in huge, choking gulps. Her voice echoed in my head over and over: *If you don't follow the rules, you will be dead.*

A thousand questions raced around my brain, like lab rats on a wheel. Where was I? How was I going to get out of here? Who were these monsters who had done this to me? But I had no answers because, as usual, no one would tell me anything. *I am so sick of being used and ignored!*

I was starting to lose it, hyperventilating so badly I was getting dizzy. *Get it together, Lucy.*

I hung my head between my knees and took slow, deep breaths until finally I felt a little calmer—and seriously thirsty. I stared at the pitcher on the crate. *Please don't let it be water.*

But of course it was water. My mother had drilled this into my head about a thousand times: "Lucy, when you're in Africa, never, ever drink any water that isn't bottled. And even then, drink it only if you open the bottle yourself."

"Why do I have to open the bottle myself?"

"Because restaurants refill the bottles with tap water and sell them as bottled. It happens all the time. And speaking of restaurants—no salads. They wash the vegetables with tap water—if they wash them at all—and you don't want to know what they use for fertilizer."

"Don't you think you're being a little paranoid?"

"Paranoid?" my mother repeated. "Not when ninety percent of all sewage in Africa is emptied into rivers and lakes without any kind of treatment. Do you really want to drink that? I'm talking about nasty things like cholera and intestinal worms. Think about it, Lucy. How would you like to pull a six-foot worm out of your intestines?"

So it was me against the parasites. Well, I was probably going to end up dead anyway, and I bet the parasites would hurt a whole lot less than whatever these people had planned for me. I raised the pitcher to my lips and paused.

Bottoms up.

Now for food. I looked down at the plate next to me. The *injera* was gray and spongy. Repulsive. I've never liked *injera*. Usually people eat it with saucy meat or vegetables on top to give it some flavor, but this was plain, with nothing to disguise the fact that *injera* feels and tastes like sour gym socks. I poked it, and my finger left a dent. *I can't eat this.* But there was nothing else.

Okay, do it fast, like pulling off a Band-Aid. I tore off a piece, and it stuck to my fingers like those steamed pork buns you get in Chinese restaurants. Except those buns are delicious. Plugging my nose with one hand, I stuffed the *injera* into my mouth with the other. *Chew, chew, chew, chew, swallow.* I gagged. Half of it was still in my throat. I swallowed again, hard, and it went down.

Eating food I hated and doing things I didn't want to do. *I really should be used to it by now. It's the story of my life.*

Chapter Seven

Three Months Ago

It was yet another of about a thousand official dinners, and I *really* hadn't wanted to go. This one was just plain weird. China had made a gift of a sports stadium to Ethiopia. The construction was almost done, and the Chinese ambassador had invited my mother and me to see the new building.

I was leaning against the doorjamb of my mother's bedroom, watching her put on makeup. *Why couldn't I have inherited any of the beautiful genes?*

"Do I really have to go to this thing? You know I'm going to be the only kid there. Besides, don't you think the Chinese could have found a better way to help Ethiopia than by building a *sports stadium*?"

She capped her lipstick. "Yes, you have to go. You know how much Ambassador Li likes you. He would be very disappointed if you weren't there. Look, Lucy, don't worry about politics. Just try to have some fun."

"Well, what am I supposed to say? 'My, what lovely seats you have!' Or 'How many stalls did you say there were in the men's room?'"

My mother tried to look stern, but I could tell she thought I was funny. Her dimples were showing. It was a dead giveaway. "Those sound like excellent and appropriate compliments. Now let's go."

Iskinder was waiting for us with the BPM. We got in back, and he took off. I stared out the window while my mother reminded me for the ten millionth time how not to act like a Neanderthal.

". . . And remember, it's not polite to refuse any food. Just take small helpings of everything they serve tonight and do your best to finish them."

Had she honestly forgotten how many of these things I'd been to in my life? And when had I ever embarrassed her? True, there was the time I got into a fistfight with that Belgian kid. But we were eight years old—and he'd started it.

 57

The stadium was in the center of the city. Tall black iron gates blocked the entrance. We cleared security and drove slowly down a long winding driveway paved with pale yellow bricks. Lining the driveway on both sides were Chinese workers wearing round flat straw hats, stationed there to greet us.

"Hey, Mom," I said, "I have a feeling we're not in Kansas anymore." She gave me a nudge.

Ambassador Li was waiting for us by the front doors with a big smile on his face. "Hello, Willa! Welcome, Lucy! I am so glad you are here tonight to see the very beautiful stadium my country has built for Ethiopia."

"And we are so happy to be here, Ming," my mother gushed. "What a wonderful gift. It will do so much to enhance the lives of the many people who use it."

Just to show I'm not such a clod after all, I shook hands with Ambassador Li Ethiopian-style—with a slight bow and my left hand holding my right forearm. I could tell he and my mother ate it up.

"Come," the ambassador said, "I will give you a tour." I followed obediently as Ambassador Li led us and the rest of the dinner guests inside the stadium.

Suddenly I noticed the music that was being piped in throughout the arena. "Excuse me, is that Elvis?"

Ambassador Li beamed. "American music in honor of our American guests." *Weirder and weirder.*

Our tour began in the arena, which, we were informed, could accommodate 15,000 spectators. "My, the seats look so comfortable, Ambassador Li!" I exclaimed. My mother gave me a warning look, and I flashed her a smile. *See how good I am?*

On our way to the prime minister's personal viewing box, we passed the restrooms. My mother shot me another look, and this time I kept my mouth shut.

When we were all seated in the box, Ambassador Li announced, "And now I have something very exciting to show my guests." He leaned over and whispered to me, "Usually I do this only for the prime minister. But tonight"—he paused for dramatic effect—"I do it"—*pause*—"for you!"

Suddenly jets of water erupted all over the field, pumping so hard they looked like fireworks.

"This is how we keep the grass healthy!" yelled Ambassador Li over the din. "The jets pump two tons of water per minute!"

Two tons of water per minute in a country where more than a million people have died in droughts. I felt sick to my stomach.

And dinner didn't help.

The dining room was large, a crazy mix of Chinese architecture, with red lacquered walls and black trim, and early-Ethiopian art in carved wood frames. Since the country is mostly Christian, all the paintings showed religious scenes, not that I recognized any of them, except for Saint George slaying the dragon. We had studied paintings like these in art class. It's kind of cool, actually. Four hundred years ago there were all these studios with artists who specialized in one tiny detail: Master of the Eyelashes, Master of the Small Chin, and my personal favorite, Master of the Sagging Cheeks.

We sat at a shiny black table in the center of the room underneath a huge gold chandelier. I looked at the endless spread of silverware and chopsticks in front of me and cringed. This was going to be a long night.

Ambassador Li clapped his hands, and on cue three waiters swept into the room carrying silver trays overflowing with food. They placed the mammoth platters on a giant lazy Susan in the middle of our table.

I'm a pretty adventurous eater, but there was stuff here I'd never seen in my life. Something pale and spongy called fish maw (I found out later that *maw* means "stomach"!) and some squiggly stuff I didn't even want to know about. Ever the dutiful daughter and under my mother's eagle eye, I put a little bit of each dish on my plate. Lucky me, I was seated next to Ambassador Li, who made sure nothing got by me. Even worse, he confessed he had a "bad stomach" (*please, spare me the details!*) and graciously sent all his portions of spicy food to me. *Maybe if I throw up all over the table, it will liven up the party—you know, make the evening memorable.*

Dr. Jonathan Clarke, from Chicago, the prime minister's personal physician, sat on my other side. I have to give him credit—he really did try: "So, Lucy, I imagine you've been to lots of places around the world in your young life. How do you like living in Ethiopia?"

"Well, to tell you the truth, Dr. Clarke," I said in between bites, "most of the time I don't feel like

I *am* living in Ethiopia. My mother doesn't let me go out on my own, and visiting museums gets a little old after a while. So mostly I just go to school and sit around at home."

Awkward silence.

"I'm, um, sorry to hear that," he said at last. "I can imagine it must be very frustrating to find yourself living in Africa and unable to experience it. Surely there must be times you get to go out and about?"

"Actually," I admitted, choking down a long piece of bok choy, "I do go on game drives sometimes."

"Really?" he said, adjusting his glasses. "Tell me about that."

"Well, there's this ranger. His name is Daniel Negash, but I call him Dahnie. He takes me into the parks, to the ones that aren't too far from Addis. He's amazing. He knows everything about all the animals, which is great for me because I'm going to be a conservation zoologist. I don't get to go as often as I want to—maybe once every two weeks or so—but I go whenever I can."

I was just getting warmed up, but Dr. Clarke wasn't listening anymore. He had turned his attention to the

German businessman seated on his other side.

Since my other dinner partner, Ambassador Li, was busy with my mother and the deputy ambassador, I was left, as usual at these things, sitting at the table with no one to talk to.

The conversation was excruciating. Listening for more than three seconds was impossible.

"It's got to be stopped before the problem gets any worse," I heard my mother say. "The United States is taking a very aggressive position."

"As you should, Madam Ambassador," said Ambassador Li. "Ethiopia has enough problems without adding this new plague."

"I agree, Ming. Poverty, famine, disease . . . One of the beautiful things about this country is that despite its overwhelming difficulties, there has been very little crime—nothing like the kind you see in Kenya or South Africa. The Ethiopian government is deeply concerned. That's why I'm cochairing the new Committee against Drug Trafficking in Ethiopia." *Wahoo! Another committee.*

I played silent games with myself to stave off boredom. *I packed my grandmother's trunk, and in it I put* **A***frica. I*

*packed my grandmother's trunk, and in it I put **A**frica and a **b**oring dinner. I packed my grandmother's trunk, and in it I put **A**frica, a **b**oring dinner, and **C**hina spending millions of dollars on a stupid stadium no one wants when it could have spent that money saving people who are dying of AIDS and starvation.*

Finally, Ambassador Li took pity on me. "Lucy, your mother says you are becoming quite a naturalist. Tell us, what is the most interesting thing you have learned so far about Ethiopian wildlife?"

I thought for a moment. "Well, Ambassador Li, I'm sure you know there are many fascinating things to learn about African mammals. For example, did you know that when female lions are in heat, they will mate every twenty minutes for as long as five days? They hardly even stop to eat!"

My mother choked on her water, and the rest of the table was stunned into silence, but out of the corner of my eye I could see Dr. Clarke grinning.

After about fifteen endless seconds Ambassador Li leaned back in his chair and slapped the table. "Ha! No wonder the lion is king of the jungle!"

The air rushed back into the room. I glanced at my mother. Her dimples were showing.

• • •

Something about this memory bothered me, like a tiny unreachable itch in the center of my back. It wasn't just the way I had felt about being forced to go to yet another boring dinner. It wasn't remembering having to gag down food I hadn't wanted to eat. It was something else. Something important . . .

The committee.

The American ambassador agrees to chair an anti-drug-trafficking committee, and three months later her daughter gets kidnapped. By drug dealers?

*I packed my grandmother's trunk, and in it I put a **dead** girl.*

Chapter Eight

Night One

My bruises ached, and a mosquito kept buzzing around my head. I named him Mr. Malaria. The good news was that whatever was in the water hadn't made me sick. Yet. It was late, after midnight, but I couldn't sleep. I kept thinking about all the things that could come crawling onto my mat, up my legs, over my face—*ugh!*

And I kept thinking about Mom and Dad. I was starting to feel pretty mad at them. How could they have put me in a situation where something like this could happen? I mean, obviously living in Ethiopia wasn't safe for me. Otherwise why would we have to live behind cement walls and razor wire?

Even though it meant getting to see African wildlife, I was totally against living in Ethiopia from the minute I'd found out we were going. Because of my parents' jobs, we've moved around my whole life—to Rome, London, Kenya, and Morocco. When I was little, I thought it was really fun and exciting to go to all these foreign countries. But when we got to Morocco, which was where we lived before coming here, I'd wanted to stay for a while. I mean, I had made really good friends in Morocco—the last thing I wanted to do was start all over again. Honestly, was it so unreasonable for someone to want to start and finish high school in the same place with the same people?

Not that my parents cared about what I wanted. This was my mother's first chance at being an ambassador, and my father was going to Indonesia to work on a huge banking-scandal thing. So they decided moving up in their careers was more important than keeping our family together. I didn't get a vote. It was one of those "this is a family, not a democracy" moments.

So, yeah, I had been really upset about not being with Dad and leaving all my friends. But even though

I had known moving to Ethiopia was a mistake, being proved right didn't feel as good as I would have expected. For one thing, getting kidnapped is a pretty high price to pay for validation. And for another, there was a not-so-tiny voice in my head telling me that part of this was my fault too.

Stupid, stupid, stupid.

I had been stupid to get in the car with Dawit. Face it, I had been stupid to sneak out in the first place. I should have known something was wrong when Dawit showed up so soon. If I had just stopped to think— or if I had trusted my gut when he first gave me the creeps—none of this would have happened. I'd have been home sleeping under my mosquito netting instead of out in the middle of nowhere probably about to die.

It was so incredibly ironic. All I'd done was complain nonstop about never being allowed out, and here I was, really out, and all I wanted was to get back in.

I hugged my knees and rocked back and forth, taking slow, deep breaths. *What are Mom and Dad doing right now? I bet they aren't sleeping either. Has Daddy gotten to*

Addis yet? Mom's probably turned the residence into a war room. I could see her in her element, giving orders, making phone calls, coordinating, dictating, managing. I could see Daddy calling all our relatives and friends. I could hear him saying, "I'm afraid I have some bad news. . . ." *Grandma Catherine and Grandpa John are going to be wrecks. What about Tana? I hope she didn't get in trouble. I hope she doesn't think what happened was her fault.*

A deep roar thundered in the distance. My head jerked up. I would know that sound anywhere: *anbasa.* A lion. Another roar. And a few minutes later, another. The last one sounded closer; it must have been a second lion answering the call of the first one.

I know a lot about lion behavior. Most people think lions roar when they're angry or when they want to show how powerful they are. But actually they do it to mark their territory and to let other lions know they're there. Lions don't want to get into fights with other lions; they roar so other lions can avoid them. Most of the time the system works pretty well. Unless food or water is scarce, and then lions go wherever they have to go to get what they need. Desperation makes them do things they wouldn't otherwise do. I guess that's true of people, too. *Is Dawit desperate? Am I?*

I once saw a whole pride of lions when I was in one of the game parks. They're called "parks," but they're not like the parks we have back home. The parks back home are meant for people, so they have benches, fountains, sculptures, playgrounds, and snack bars. Even the big ones—like Rock Creek Park in D.C.—are small enough to walk around in a day.

The game parks in Africa are about land and animals that the government is supposed to protect from developers and poachers. The Menagesha National Park, which is the one closest to Addis, is considered small even though it's four hundred square miles. When you're inside, the land and the sky go on forever, and it's so beautiful you never want to leave. It's hard to put into words, but Africa is the only place I've ever been where human beings feel like just one small part of a vast and complicated earth.

When I'm in the bush, my favorite view is an acacia tree—or, even better, a grove of them—silhouetted against the blue sky in a wide-open field of tall grass. Acacias are the trees everyone thinks of when they think of Africa, the ones that look like umbrellas because of their long thin trunks and wide canopies. Actually, that's what people call them: umbrella trees. Sometimes I stretch my arms, reaching my fingers out as far as they can go, and tilt my head way back so I see nothing but endless sky. I sway slowly side to side, feeling the grass gently brush against my legs, and pretend I am an acacia tree. It's as close as I ever get to believing in God.

• • •

"Did you see any warthogs today?" I asked Dahnie one morning not too long ago. We were driving around Menagesha National Park, looking for anything and everything, like always. I love warthogs. With their giant snouts and beady little eyes, they're the ugliest animals on the planet, and I laugh every time I see one.

"Oh yes, Lucy, I told them you were coming today. They said to tell you *chhhhh!*" He made a huge snorting noise, and I cracked up. Dahnie can be a total goofball even if he is twenty-five years old and married. Dahnie is superskinny and about the same height as my mother, which is about average for an

Ethiopian man. Because nutrition is so bad here, people are much smaller and thinner than people back home. For once I fit right in.

I love going on game drives. Not just because of the animals but also because it's the only time I really feel free to just be who I am and do what matters to me. It was a gorgeous morning, even cool enough for me to wear a sweatshirt. I took a deep breath and let the air come whooshing out. "So," I asked Dahnie, "where to first?"

"I thought we would head west a bit. I want to check on some blue-winged geese that are nesting in the grass."

He waited while I checked my watch: 9:44 here and 1:44 in Bethesda. The compass showed we were headed north. I pointed left. "Thataway," I said.

We bounced along the dusty road for a while, not saying much. Dahnie's rifle rested on the seat between us, but I was used to it, since Dahnie always carried it with him when we were in the park. *"You never know what can happen out in the bush, Lucy."* Dahnie's father was killed by poachers when Dahnie was very young. Sometimes I watch Dahnie and look for that loss, but I never see it. I only see the peace he and I share when we're in the park. The sadness and anger must be buried somewhere deep.

The jeep bumped over the rocks, and I gazed out the open window at the tall grasses and bushy olive trees. We stopped and got out of the car to watch a herd of antelope grazing in the distance. I plucked a grass stem and chewed it for a while, fantasizing.

"They're so beautiful," I said at last. "Wouldn't it be amazing to walk right in there with them?"

"Do not forget, Lucy, they are wild animals. You must respect their need for distance from you."

"Oh, Dahnie, why do you always have to remind me how dangerous everything is?"

"I do not try to scare you, Lucy. I want you to understand your place in this park and to respect the animals that live here."

"You know I respect them," I said, "but can't I also *admire* them? Can't I *wish* that things were different and I didn't have to worry about them eating me and they didn't have to worry about me shooting them?"

Dahnie laughed. "Of course you can."

We got back into the car and continued driving.

"Dahnie?"

"Yes, Lucy?"

"What did Ethiopia look like before? I mean before so many of the trees were cut down."

"It was much more green, of course. But there was also much more of everything—more fertile soil, more animals, more rain. Deforestation is terrible for Ethiopia. It makes a very bad cycle of poverty and famine. Without trees, the earth dries up, the wells dry up. Then the farmers cannot grow food, and their animals cannot graze. The wild animals die too, because they also do not have enough food. It is as bad as war."

"So why does the government let people keep chopping down trees?"

"What else can the people do? They are so poor they cannot buy other fuel. The government plants more trees, but people cut them down faster than the government can plant them."

Suddenly Dahnie slammed on the breaks so hard I almost smashed my head on the dashboard.

"Over there," he said in a fierce whisper. "Look there, Lucy."

I looked first at him and then out the window where he was pointing.

I gasped.

There in the shade of a huge acacia, maybe twenty feet away from us, sat a whole pride. I counted them. Two lionesses, three cubs, and several yards away from the rest of the group, a full-grown lion.

We were so lucky. Most of the big game in Ethiopia has been poached or, like Dahnie said, has died off from deforestation. There are maybe a thousand wild lions left in the whole country. We watched them for a long time. The male seemed to be sleeping. The cubs played a lot, and the lionesses mostly ignored them.

"Dahnie?"

"Yes, Lucy?"

"How come they just sit there?"

He turned to face me. "Why should they get up?"

"What do you mean, 'Why should they get up'?" I asked.

"I mean just what I said. Why should they get up? What do they need to do? They have no predators, so they do not need to be on the lookout for anyone."

"But don't they have to go find food or something?

I don't know—don't they need exercise?" It just seemed bizarre to me that wild animals could have so much leisure time.

"A lion can eat one hundred pounds of meat at one meal and then eat very little for a week. Lions sleep as much as twenty hours in a day." Dahnie paused, like he always does before he says something he wants me to remember.

"Lions are the most powerful members of the animal kingdom. They do not get up, Lucy, because they do not have to."

• • •

All alone in my shack, I thought about that for a long time. *What makes a lion have to get up? What makes anyone take action?*

Chapter Nine

Day Two

The lions roared on and off all night, and I stayed awake listening to them. Then it hit me—I knew where I was! Well, sort of. Almost all the lions in Ethiopia are in the southern and southwestern parts of the country. If there were lions nearby, that was where I had to be. For the first time I felt as if I was *somewhere* instead of *anywhere*. I was no longer adrift in a million square miles in the Horn of Africa. Instead, I was lost in one finite region that I could picture on a map in my mind. My newfound knowledge felt like a small anchor that tethered me to a familiar reality. It comforted me just enough that I could fall asleep.

I woke up to voices outside my jail cell again.

Sunlight streaming through the cracks in the walls told me it was morning.

"English, please! There will be no Amharic here. We speak a language all three of us understand, or we don't speak at all." It was the woman who had brought me the *injera*. She was definitely British. She had one of those boarding school accents that I could recognize anywhere—I had met enough of those girls.

And she had just confirmed that the men were speaking Amharic, so my initial hypothesis was proved correct: I had been kidnapped by greater than or equal to two Ethiopian men—and one British woman.

In the morning light I could see my prison much better. It looked like something that had just been thrown together, maybe even something temporary. There were spaces where the boards didn't line up all the way and sunlight poured through, so I knew it was a freestanding building and not part of a larger house. I got up off the mat slowly because of my painful bruises and as quietly as possible so they wouldn't hear me and put my eye up to one of the biggest cracks. I could see the woman, half of a man's back . . . and Dawit.

"Be patient, Dawit. Let them worry about the girl.

It will make our position stronger." The other man turned as he spoke, and I recognized him as the man with the bad teeth from the car. Unlike Dawit, who was tall and beefy by Ethiopian standards (in other words, average by American standards), Nasty Teeth was small and wiry. He reminded me of a mole viper, a little black snake that looks harmless but you don't want to get it mad because one bite will kill you.

"No, Markos, Dawit is right," the woman said. "You need to make the call now." *Markos. Nasty Teeth's name is Markos.*

"Are you giving orders, Helena?" *Helena.* "That is not your job here." Markos sounded annoyed.

"No, it isn't my job, is it?" she said.

"Enough!" Markos snapped. "I will call when the time is right. You will do nothing until I say so. And, Dawit, remember that as far as the police know, *you* are the only person connected to this event. I wonder how many people are looking for you right now."

"You would not dare," Dawit said, so quietly I could barely hear him.

I held my breath in the long moment of silence that followed.

"Just be patient, my friends," Markos said at last, condescension dripping in his voice.

A car door slammed, and I heard the crunch of dirt and gravel as the car drove away.

Despite the sweltering heat, my whole body felt icy. I had a very bad feeling about Markos. He seemed like the meanest one of the three, and he also seemed to be the one in control—not a good combination.

I paced back and forth in the small space, fuming. Whoever they were, if these people thought they could just sit around and take their sweet time dealing with this, then they didn't have a clue about the way things worked in the world. They had kidnapped the daughter of the United States ambassador. My mother wasn't going to just wait politely for *Markos* to decide when it would be a good time to talk. She'd make sure they got sent to jail for life after pulling a stunt like this.

Then I began to wonder. I'd heard that a huge number of marriages in Ethiopia take place by abduction. Sometimes the girls are even younger than me. I couldn't begin to imagine why or how that could happen. Would things really be different for me because I'm an *American* girl?

.   .   .

One of my favorite places to visit in Addis—okay, one of the only places I'm allowed to visit in Addis, but I would like it no matter what—is the National Museum. That's where the other Lucy lives, the one who's more than three million years old and whose skeleton is the most complete human ancestor ever discovered. They keep her in the basement of the museum, in this out-of-the-way section that looks like a shabby old rec room with cheap wood paneling and faded industrial carpet. You know where she is only because someone printed "Lucy Room" in thick black letters on regular computer paper and thumbtacked the sign to the wall over the doorway. Every time I see Lucy, she blows me away. She's so tiny and old, and yet we're the same— same name, same number of bones, same upright walk. I just sit on this rickety wooden stool they have in the room and stare at her and wonder.

Upstairs at the museum there's another skull from the same kind of hominid as Lucy. I asked the curator once why that skull was twice as big as hers. He explained that the skull upstairs was male. "Back then, miss, humans were more like apes, and so the males were much bigger than the females, almost twice as big."

"Wow, I had no idea," I said.

"You do not know about it because Western people do not like to think their ancestors came from Africa. Western people want to believe they are very different from African people. But they are wrong. It does not matter whether you are African or American, Christian or Muslim. Nationality and religion are just politics. We are all one species."

• • •

All one species. Except we don't always treat each other that way, do we? My mental ramblings were cut short when Helena showed up with my breakfast. Her jaw was clenched, and she looked even paler than she had the night before.

"Here," she said, handing me another plate of *injera.* She checked my water jug to see if it was empty.

"You should drink more. You don't want to get dehydrated in this heat."

I didn't tell her I was trying to maintain a delicate balance between the amount of water and the number of parasites in my system.

"Helena, I heard you talking before. Why haven't you called my parents yet?"

"I told you already," she snapped. "You don't need to know."

Helena picked up my bucket. "I'm going to empty this. I'll bring you some leaves that you can use for loo paper when I come back with the bucket." An empty bucket and some leaves. It was ridiculous how happy that made me.

Helena. I bet that wasn't even her real name. Was Helena the name of one of her friends or a relative? Or maybe someone in a book? Knowing where she got the name might tell me something about her. My dad, who's an opera fanatic, named me Lucy for his favorite opera heroine, Lucia di Lammermoor. I thought it was kind of romantic to be named after an opera heroine until my parents finally took me to see the opera at La Scala in Italy when I was ten. That's when I found out Lucia is this completely oppressed girl who gets forced into marriage with a guy she doesn't love, goes crazy, and kills her husband. I asked my father if my name reflected his hopes and dreams for me, but he just laughed and said, "Stop being so precocious. Opera is about the glory of the music, not the silliness of the story."

My favorite Lucy is Lucy from the Narnia Chronicles. *The Lion, the Witch, and the Wardrobe* is one of my all-time favorite books, even though I'm kind of too old for it now. I must have read the whole series at least nine or ten times.

I wish I could be Lucy from Narnia. I wish a huge talking lion would come and rescue me.

Chapter Ten

After Helena left, I wolfed down my *injera* and about half of my water and got down to business. *Okay, Dian, let's investigate our surroundings.* First I tried the door, but of course it was locked. Then I checked the compass on my watch and headed over to the north wall of the room, the one Dawit, Helena, and Markos had been standing near. With them out of the way I could see across a football field of tall grass all the way to a fairly dense wooded area. The cracks on the east wall showed more of the same, and south was just grass and scrubby bushes. But when I looked west, I saw another building about twenty feet from mine. It had the same tin roof, but it looked a little bigger. I guessed that must be where Dawit, Helena, and Markos were staying. Outside their hut I could see three dogs sleeping in the dirt, two brown ones and a black one. They were the kind of skinny, mangy, medium-size dogs you see running around a lot of the villages, and they'll rip your throat out in seconds if they think you've got something they can eat. Luckily, they were chained to a metal post.

With nothing more to explore, I lay down on my mat. The hours crawled by. The heat was stifling. Sweat trickled down my back and the sides of my face. Some of it got in my eyes, which turned out to be a good thing because the sweat helped loosen my contact lenses, which felt like gritty suction cups. After twenty-four hours with no soap and no toothbrush I felt absolutely filthy, and I'm sure I smelled even worse, but those were the least of my problems.

The heat must have been getting to the animals, too, because it was totally silent outside. No lions or birds. No wind at all. Even the flies and the mosquitoes were resting. But I was too jittery to rest. I tried counting prime numbers to a thousand and then making an alphabetical list of all the mammals that are endemic to sub-Saharan Africa (*aardvark, aardwolf, Abbott's duiker*)—anything to keep from thinking about what was happening to me—but nothing worked.

I was lying on my back on the straw mat, busy calculating the percentage of the total surface area of the hut that each piece of wallboard made up, with a unit of measurement equaling one forearm, when the roar of a car motor broke the silence. I jumped up and ran to the opposite wall to peer through one of the cracks. Within seconds I saw Markos and Dawit pull up to the front of their hut in an old jeep. The dogs started barking, and Helena ran outside as the men were getting out of the car, screaming at each other in Amharic.

"What's going on?" she demanded. "What's happened?"

"The Americans, they will not negotiate." *What??!* "They will not even listen to the demands," Dawit said. "They say we must release the girl immediately."

"There! You see? I told you we shouldn't have waited to call them," Helena accused, "but you wouldn't listen."

"Stay out of it!" That was Markos. He raised his

hand like he was going to smack Helena, and for the first time I noticed the rifle hanging from a strap over his left shoulder. My gut twisted.

"I will not stay out of it," she shouted back, ignoring Markos's hand, which was now down at his side and clenched in a fist. "You know we only have three more days." *Three more days???* "And then what? Have you thought about that? What are we going to do then?"

All the screaming was driving the dogs insane. It was hard to hear anything over their barking.

Helena pointed at Markos. "I knew you would screw this up!"

"I did not *screw up* anything," Markos shot back. "They do not mean what they say. They will negotiate. The American government will not let the ambassador's daughter die." *Die?!*

"They let that journalist die," Dawit said.

"That was terrorism."

"And this is so different?" Dawit asked, his voice bitter.

"Of course it is," said Helena. "You know that. This is a business transaction. A business transaction that Markos has so far managed to botch, I might add."

Markos lunged for Helena, and everything turned into complete chaos. Dawit held Markos back, and the three of them kept yelling at each other while the dogs barked furiously. Finally, Markos shook off Dawit and shouted, "Quiet!"

My captors went silent, but the animals kept barking like crazy. I stared openmouthed as Markos stomped over and kicked the black dog, hard, in the head. There was a sickening crack like dry wood snapping, and the black dog flopped to the ground while the brown ones cowered together, whining.

Markos glared. "Bring it to the forest. The hyenas will take care of it."

My hands were shaking so hard I had to ball them into fists to make them stop. I scrunched up my face and held my breath to keep from crying out. I couldn't believe what I had just seen. Markos had killed that dog like it was nothing.

The Americans won't negotiate. No way. I refused to believe it. Mom and Dad would never, ever, *ever* give up trying to get me back. If the Americans weren't negotiating, it was because Mom couldn't, not because she wouldn't. Which meant . . . which meant I was probably right about the drug traffickers and this *was* about something more than just money.

They're never going to let me out of here alive.

I watched Dawit drag the black dog by its hind legs all the way to the trees. When he passed my hut, he looked anguished. But by the time he returned, he must have pulled himself together because his face had no expression at all.

Helena paced back and forth in front of her hut. When Dawit came back, he jerked his head in a "let's go" gesture. They walked off together in silence.

The afternoon crawled by until about six o'clock, when Helena showed up with my dinner. I decided I had nothing to lose.

"Helena, please talk to me. Please tell me what's going on."

No answer.

"Please, Helena. Markos is crazy. Why don't you and Dawit and I just go? I promise I'll get my parents to help you. I swear I will." Now the words came pouring out. I was saying anything, anything at all, to save myself—or at least to get her to give me some hope.

"Helena, my parents won't be mad at you if you bring me home. They'll do whatever you want to get me back."

Helena finished filling my water jug and turned to go. I was frantic.

"Why me?" I pleaded. "Can you just tell me that one thing? Why me? What did I do?"

But before she could answer, the door smashed open. It was Dawit, his face livid.

"What did I do?" he whined, imitating me. "Poor little girl. Such terrible problems you have." He glared at me for a second, about to go on, but then he seemed to change his mind.

"I will tell you a story about another girl just like you," he said, his voice tight and angry. His quiet fury scared me way more than shouting would have.

"Her name was Maryam. She lived in a small village with her mother and father, her younger brother, and her sister, who was only a baby. Every day Maryam's father worked in the field next to their *tukul,* trying to grow food to feed his family." Dawit paced back and forth while he spoke. Helena stood frozen, listening to him. "But there was almost no rain that year, and so there was very little food. All of the people in the village were hungry." He paused. "The pump in the village could give no more water, so Maryam walked very far every day to bring water to her family. The water she found was filthy, and the family knew it, but what choice did they have?" He paused again and let out a deep breath before continuing. "No one in the village had a choice. And many people became sick from the bad water and because they were starving." Dawit's voice had grown so quiet it was almost a whisper. I was afraid to move a muscle.

"Maryam's brother became sick. Their father carried him ten kilometers to the health clinic, but by the time they got there, no medicine was left. And so Maryam's father carried her brother back, sicker than before, and when they got home, Maryam's brother was dead." Dawit had stopped pacing. He stared over my shoulder as if all the people in the story were ghosts that only he could see.

"Very soon Maryam's sister became sick, and then her mother. They all died. Many people died that year—like they do every year in Africa. This is a very common story." Dawit stopped and looked at me with a challenge in his eyes, like it was my turn to say something.

"What happened to Maryam? Is she still living in the same village with her father?"

"I am Maryam's father. She is dead. "

I thought about Teddy's face every time something reminded him of his brothers. Dawit had lost his entire family. I didn't know what to say.

"I'm very sorry about your family, Dawit," I said softly. "But, well, I don't understand what it has to do with me."

"What does it have to do with you?" Dawit repeated, shaking his head with a bitter smile. "Nothing," he spit out. "It has *nothing* to do with you, Lucy." He paused. "And *that* is the problem with Africa."

They left, and I just stood with my face in my hands in the middle of the floor, whispering "I want to go home, I want to go home" over and over again like a prayer.

"Lucy." It was Markos.

He grabbed hold of my trembling shoulders and leaned so close to me I could feel his breath against my ear. "That was not very smart," he hissed.

Markos stood up straight, and I flinched at the hatred in his eyes.

Wham! He smacked me hard across my face with the back of his hand. I kept my head facing the wall and managed to hold back my tears just until he was gone.

Chapter Eleven

Night Two

I lay curled up in a ball on my mat, staring at the opening near the ceiling, unable to sleep. Mr. Malaria was back, and he'd brought some friends, but I was beyond caring. I wasn't even hungry anymore. *Who puts a window near a ceiling, where no one can see out? They probably just ran out of scrap wood and didn't care about filling the gap.*

There's an old spiritual my mother used to sing to me whenever I was really upset, called "Hush." It's all about Jesus, which is kind of funny because my family isn't religious at all. But Mom loves religious music for its beauty, whether it's Handel or gospel. I've always loved the song, especially the "hush, hush" part.

Hush, hush, somebody's callin' my name.
Oh my Lord, oh my Lord, what can I do?
Sounds like Jesus, somebody's callin' my name.
Oh my Lord, oh my Lord, what can I do?
Soon one morning, death come creepin' at my room.

Oh my God. I'd never really thought much about the words before. I'd better not be having some kind of premonition.

Oh my Lord, oh my Lord, what can I do?

The opening. It was so small and high up, my captors had probably never even thought of putting in bars or boarding it up. *I wonder . . .*

Very quietly I placed the lantern on the floor and carried the crate to the wall directly under the opening. Standing on top of the crate, I reached up as high as I could. My fingers were maybe four inches from the bottom of the gap. I was pretty sure that if I jumped, I could get a good grip on the board and pull myself through. I had done much harder jumps in my gymnastics classes. It would be tight, but I thought I could do it. For once in my life it was good to be a runt.

Yeah, but then what? I knew that the minute I got outside, the dogs would start barking and it would be all over. I could never outrun them, especially not barefoot. And even if I got lucky and the dogs didn't bark and I got away, where would I go? I didn't even know where I was, let alone how to find someplace else. And like Helena had said, if the dogs didn't get me, the hyenas would. Or the lions. I was trapped.

That's it. I'm trapped, and I'm never getting out alive, and there's nothing I can do about it. It's the same old stupid story, whether it's the cement walls at the residence or this damn hut. THERE'S NOTHING I CAN DO ABOUT IT.

I thought about what Tana had said on our way to the *mercato*. For once in my life I wanted to be able to *do* something. I wanted to make a decision for myself and act on it.

Well, right there, right then, there was only one choice I could make: *If I can't choose how I get to live, at least I can choose how I get to die.* And maybe, just maybe, there was a .00001 percent chance I'd get lucky.

If Jane, Dian, and Biruté could take leaps into the unknown, so could I. *All right, ladies, time for a little planning.*

I moved the crate back to its usual spot and sat down on my mat to think.

Major Obstacles to My Escape
1. Dawit, Helena, and Markos
2. Dogs
3. No shoes
4. No food
5. No water
6. Insect bites
7. Snakes
8. Wild animals
9. No idea where I'm going

How to Deal with These Obstacles
1. Dawit, Helena, and Markos—*I'll leave when they're away, or at least inside. If I get a good head start, I should be able to hide from them in the woods.*
2. Dogs—*Luckily, the window is on the wall farthest from the dogs, and the dogs are chained. I'll escape when they're sleeping. If Dawit, Helena, and Markos release them to chase me, I'm probably dead meat. Literally.*
3. No shoes—*Nothing I can do.*

4. No food—*Stockpile injera, hope to find berries or nuts that I recognize as nonpoisonous. Bugs are an absolute, on-death's-doorstep last resort.*

5. No water—*Since I can't carry it, I'll have to find a water source like a stream or a watering hole. If I'm south of Addis and not southwest, there may be a lake nearby.*

6. Insect bites—*Nothing I can do. Try not to scratch.*

7. Snakes—*There aren't too many poisonous ones in Ethiopia, but if I climb any trees, I need to remember to check for pythons.*

8. Wild animals—*Avoid at all costs! Lions and leopards sleep most of the day, so I'll leave in the morning. If I have to spend the night out there, I'll follow the advice Dahnie always gave me: "Walking around in the wild at night is just asking for trouble. It is much better to spend the night in a tree."*

9. No idea where I'm going—*Since I was unconscious for about six hours, my best guess is I'm within two hundred miles south or southwest of Addis. I'll head north and keep my fingers crossed.*

Once I was at a rhino preserve feeding sugarcane to a white rhino when the rhino turned around, stamped his foot a few times, and peed all over me. It was totally disgusting, but later Iskinder told me rhino pee brings good luck. I hoped he wasn't kidding.

I lay down and tried to sleep, but my mind was racing. I kept thinking about Iskinder and how I had lied to him at Tana's. *"I promise I won't do anything I shouldn't do."* I cringed. Iskinder is the only person in my life who makes any effort to actually spend time with me—all the lunches and dinners and those hours building card houses. He's never been anything but kind to me, and look how I treated him. Iskinder. A man who has lived among kings. And me, who am I? Just some bratty American kid.

. . .

From 1930 until 1974, His Imperial Majesty Haile Selassie I, King of Kings and Lord of Lords, Conquering Lion of the Tribe of Judah, was emperor of Ethiopia. And from 1968 until 1974, Iskinder was Selassie's pillow bearer, just as his father had been before him.

Iskinder told me about it one day while we were building Selassie's Jubilee Palace out of cards.

"You were his *what*?" I couldn't believe my ears.

 100

"I was His Majesty's pillow bearer."

"But what does that *mean*, Iskinder? What does a pillow bearer *do*?" I had visions of Iskinder tucking Haile Selassie into bed at night, fluffing mountains of frilly pillows.

"Well, you see, Lucy, the emperor was not a large man. In fact, he was not much taller than you. But of course it is only proper that a man so exalted in position be seated far above his subjects. For this reason, all of the imperial thrones in the palace were built high off the ground."

"But what does that have to do with pillows?" I gently placed a jack of clubs on top of Selassie's bathroom to make a ceiling.

"Think of it, Lucy. Just imagine how it would look if important men came to see the emperor and he sat on his throne with his feet swinging back and forth like a child. No, it would not do at all. It would not be dignified."

"So what did you do?"

"My job was to quickly place a pillow under the feet of His Majesty as he sat down so that his feet would not dangle in the air for even a moment."

I nearly knocked over the our replica of Selassie's indoor lion cages. Could Iskinder be making this up? But, no, his face looked perfectly serious.

"I remember one morning not long after I had begun my job in the palace—the kitchen wall, Lucy, it needs more support." I propped it up with a two of diamonds and Iskinder continued. "I was a young man, maybe about the same age as your friend Dahnie. A small group of important men from Kenya had come to propose a cultural exchange program.

"Emperor Selassie was already seated on his throne, his feet resting upon the proper pillow, when the men entered the audience chamber. As the Kenyan dignitaries stood before the throne offering their deepest appreciation for His Gracious Majesty's kindness and indulgence, His Highness's little dog jumped off his lap and ran about, as she always did on such occasions."

"Selassie had a dog?" I interrupted.

"Oh, yes, Lucy. Her name was Lulu, like your father's nickname for you. The emperor loved her very much. She slept in his bed every night and traveled with him always. However . . . Lulu was not so well trained."

I looked sharply at Iskinder and saw the tiniest hint of a smile on his face. The story was about to get good, I could tell. I stopped building.

"As I said, Lulu ran around the men's feet. And then, about halfway through their presentation, Lulu urinated on one of the men's shoes."

"She did *what!*"

"Oh, it was not at all uncommon. In truth, Lulu urinated on visitors' feet nearly every day. Of course, the esteemed gentlemen had to pretend they did not notice. It would have been the height of disrespect to draw one's attention from the emperor himself or to suggest that his dog was ill behaved."

"So all of them just had to stand there with pee on their shoes?"

"Oh no, Lucy. That would be dishonorable for the visitors." Iskinder leaned back to consider the throne room that he had just completed. It included a seven of hearts we had covered with tin foil to make it look like Selassie's huge wall mirror, one that Iskinder told me had special distorting glass to make the emperor look taller. Satisfied, he started working on another audience chamber. "No, Fasilidas would step in immediately and wipe the urine from the men's shoes with a purple satin cloth."

"Wait. I'm sorry, Iskinder, I just have to make sure I understand you. Are you saying there was a man at the palace whose job was to wipe dog pee off dignitaries' shoes?"

"That is correct. Fasilidas was keeper of the cloth for ten years." Iskinder held up two cards and rubbed them together. "Am I going to build this palace all by myself?"

"I'm sorry. This is all just so wild! You were pillow bearer, Fasilidas was keeper of the cloth. What other jobs did people have at the palace?"

"Well, perhaps the most powerful position was minister of the pen."

I could just see it: a man in a little room surrounded by cups with pens of every variety—ballpoint, fountain, felt-tip, quill . . .

"Okay, I'll bite. What did the all-powerful minister of the pen do?"

"Now you will begin to understand the wisdom of King Haile Selassie. You see, Lucy, although the

emperor was able to read and to write, he never did
so. Never. Instead, all documents were read to him,
and all his orders were transcribed by the minister of
the pen. And His Highness was just as careful with his
speech. When His Majesty spoke, it was in a whisper
so quiet his lips barely moved, and the minister of the
pen had to put his ear inches from the emperor's lips
in order to hear him."

"But why would he do that? Didn't he worry that
people would think he couldn't read?"

"Ah, Lucy, you are thinking like a modern American
girl. The literacy of His Most Unparalleled Highness,
the Supreme Chosen One, was not of primary
importance to his subjects. What do you think would
be more important?" Now Iskinder stopped building.

"I don't know."

"Think, Lucy."

"Um, infallibility?"

"Yes, go on."

"Power?"

"Exactly! If Emperor Selassie used the minister
of the pen to speak for him, he could always blame
anything that did not go well on the minister's

getting it wrong. When things did go well, His Royal Highness could take all the credit."

"You talk about Selassie with so much respect, Iskinder. But what about how he wouldn't let most people own any land? And how he let all those people die during the big drought because he was too embarrassed to ask the rest of the world for help?"

"That is true, Lucy. But Ethiopia is a proud country. Yes, we were occupied by the Italians during the Second World War, but we are still the only country in Africa that has never been colonized. Emperor Selassie was a symbol of our independence. Did you know that at one time he was the longest-serving ruler in the world? That meant if he was in a room with other heads of state—other presidents, kings, and prime ministers—he was treated as the most important person there. You see, even though we are a democracy now, for many people life is harder today than it was forty years ago, during Selassie's reign. Nothing is simple, Lucy." Iskinder's voice drifted off, and he stared at our finished work.

"It was a very beautiful palace," he said quietly, almost as though he had forgotten I was there. With a flick of his index finger he knocked over a king of diamonds, sending all the other cards fluttering down after it.

. . .

Iskinder was right. Nothing is simple.

Why can the lion lie unafraid in the grass? Why does a man spend his days on his knees cleaning dog urine off other men's shoes? Why does an adult tolerate the rudeness of a child?

Why kidnap an American girl in Ethiopia?

Power.

Chapter Twelve

Day Three

The beams of early-morning light crisscrossing the room were so beautiful I could almost forget the ugliness of my situation. Almost, but not quite. The beauty was shattered by the cold, hard fact of E-Day, Escape Day. I had to get ready. I sat up carefully, because my bruises still hurt. My contacts felt worse than ever, and I rubbed my eyes to loosen them.

No.

One of my lenses popped out. *No, no, no!*

I froze, knowing the worst thing I could do was move quickly and risk stepping on it or flinging it from wherever it had fallen. I'm so nearsighted that even with one lens still in, I can hardly see. For a full minute I sat perfectly still, my eyes squeezed shut, panicking. *This isn't happening. I can't get away if I can't see.* I had to find it.

Very slowly I examined my lap and the area around me on the mat. Nothing. Without moving my feet, I leaned over and looked around the dirt floor. Still nothing. Choking back tears of frustration, I searched the dirt inch by inch, patting the ground in front of me, my nose practically in the dust. I looked like one of those truffle-sniffing pigs. All I could think about was the inside of my medicine cabinet at the residence and the boxes of extra lenses stacked neatly on the third shelf. It's so easy at home. You lose something and, no big deal, you just grab another.

There! It was underneath the edge of the mat. How it had gotten there, I'd never know, but I didn't care. I just felt so incredibly relieved to have it back. I looked it over carefully. It wasn't torn, but the lens was already a little dried out, and one side was covered with dirt. There was no way I could put that thing back in my eye the way it was.

Fine. So I had a choice: spit or water. *Do parasites attack your eyeballs or just your intestines? God, I can't believe I'm*

in a situation where I even have to ask that question.

I chose water. At least that way I wouldn't end up eating the dirt that was on the lens and adding to all the other microbes that were already partying in my digestive system. I poured some water from the jug over my fingers and rubbed the lens to get the dirt off. My eye doctor had told me many times never to rinse my lenses with anything but sterile saline. Ha! *This is going to kill.*

It killed, all right. Like a hundred little toothpicks jabbing the underside of my eyelid. My eye started tearing like crazy, but I resisted the overwhelming urge to get the thing *out* of my eye, hoping my tears would wash away the tap water and what was left of the dirt.

And, thank God, it worked. After several agonizing minutes the worst of the pain was gone, and I could function. E-day was back on.

There wasn't a lot I could do to get ready. Since I couldn't carry it with me, I drank all the water that was left in the jug. Who knew how long it would take me to find a water source? I wanted to be maximally hydrated before I left. I ate half of the *injera* I had saved from the night before. I would bring the other half with me—plus whatever Helena gave me this morning. Now all I could do was wait. Wait for the dogs to go to sleep and for my jailers to get out of the way.

• • •

"You have a bruise on your face."

It was 9:33, and Helena had come with my breakfast. I touched my cheek gently and winced. Amazing—with everything that had been going on, I hadn't even noticed.

"Yeah."

"I wish I had ice or something cold, but there isn't any electricity here."

"Whatever."

Helena put the *injera* on the crate. She stared at me like there was something she wanted to say but she wasn't sure she should say it.

"It wasn't supposed to be like this."

"Really? How was it supposed to be?"

"Quick. You were supposed to be on your way home by now."

I shrugged. "It's not really my home."

"No, I suppose it's not," she conceded.

"It's not your home either, Helena."

 III

I waited for her to say something, but she didn't.

"Just out of curiosity, what are you doing in this country, anyway?"

She paused before answering me. "I work here."

"What are you, some kind of aid worker or teacher or something?" A kidnapping English teacher didn't seem likely, but teaching and aid work are the kinds of jobs most white women tend to have in this country.

"No, I came to Ethiopia for business. Regrettably, your government has created some obstacles."

"Oh, I get it. So you figured kidnapping me would be the best way to remove those obstacles." I nodded my head like I was thinking it over. "And how's that working for you?"

"Don't talk about things you don't understand," she snapped. "And watch the way you speak to me."

"Oh, I understand all right," I said, ignoring her warning. I had already seen that her tough-girl act was mostly just for show. "I know exactly what you're up to. I know all about the committee. And I also know that Markos is a psycho and you've totally lost control of the situation."

"Committee?" Helena snorted, a scornful little

British sniff. She squatted down by my mat so she could look at me eye to eye. "You're a very smart little girl, aren't you, Lucy? You think you have it all figured out. Well, you don't. There is no *committee,* and I should think that by now you'd understand that I really don't care whether you go home to your mum and dad."

No committee? Was she for real or just covering up? I couldn't tell.

"And what about Dawit? What does he care about?"

"I expect he's in this for the same reason I am: money."

Helena stood up to leave. When she got halfway out the door, I stopped her. "So how much am I worth?" I held her gaze.

"We'll find out," she said.

Chapter Thirteen

If I'd had any doubts before about my decision to escape, they were gone now. One thing I knew for sure: My mother may have been impossible and hugely disappointed in me, but if this were just about ransom, my parents would have given them anything. But taking on the government? Committee or no committee, they underestimated what it would take to get the United States to give in to the demands of kidnappers. *The lion isn't going to get up for one spoiled little girl, even if she is the American ambassador's daughter.*

I had to face facts: Nobody was going to come for me, and I couldn't wait any longer. The dogs were asleep, and Dawit, Helena, and Markos were in their shack. I needed to get out early, while I still had plenty of time to find . . . whatever I could find. *Don't think; just do.*

I stuffed the *injera* into my pants pockets and drank the last of the water Helena had brought with breakfast. I peered through the cracks in the walls one more time to make sure the dogs were sleeping and Markos, Helena, and Dawit were inside. My eye was still tearing from what was left of the dirt on my contact, but I could see the coast was clear.

I picked up the crate and carefully set it down under the opening, digging it into the dirt a little so it wouldn't slip when I jumped. I was going to have to jump as high as I could to get a good hold on the top of the board and then pull myself through. *God, I better fit.*

I jumped once, too cautiously, and didn't make the grab. Clearly, reaching that space was going to take more of an effort than I had thought. I squatted down low to give myself better leverage and leaped as high as I could, smashing my knee into the wall in the process. Swallowing a scream of pain, I held my breath and counted to ten, waiting for someone to notice the huge thud that my knee had just made. But for once, luck was on my side.

Next time I jumped strong and straight. *One, two . . . Made it!* My fingers dug into the rough wood, but I ignored the sting, pausing for a second to fully appreciate the bizarreness of my situation: There I was, dangling from a tin-roofed shack in rural Ethiopia, making my escape from captivity to almost certain death. Tana was probably in her room listening to her iPod right now. Teddy was probably napping under a tree or something. My parents . . . I couldn't think about my parents. *Don't think; just do.*

I took a deep breath and pulled myself up as hard as I could, trying to walk my feet up the wall. It didn't work. I wasn't strong enough. All I could think about was my complaining about doing chin-ups in gym because "we'll never have to do anything like this in real life, so what's the point?" *Boy, if there is a God, he sure does have a sense of humor.*

But I wasn't going to give up. After all, this was the easy part, right? *One, two, three.* Walk-walk-walk-walk up the wall. *Yes!* My head and shoulders were hanging outside, but the opening was too small for me to wriggle all the way through. *Okay, not a problem. I'm flexible.* I gave another little prayer of thanks for all those years of gymnastics classes. Pulling back a bit, I slipped one arm through, then my head, and then the other arm, almost like doing the front crawl in a swimming pool. Now half my body, from the waist up, was hanging outside. My hips are so narrow it should have been easy to slide the rest of me out.

Except that I'm an idiot. A complete and total idiot. I was about to slide face first out a hole six feet off the ground! Somehow I had to get my feet out first. *Okay, Lucy, you can do this.*

I inched back into the cabin until I was hanging onto the board by my hands again, with my knees bent and my feet pressed against the wall. All of a sudden one of the dogs let out a squeal, and the other one answered it with a growl. *Damn!* I jumped to the ground and crouched down, anxiously tapping my fingers on the dirt floor.

Six endless minutes later the dogs were quiet, and I felt pretty sure no one was coming to see what had disturbed them. I started over: stepped onto the crate, leaped up to grab the board, and this time walked my feet up the wall between my arms and through the opening. It was almost like hanging upside down on the monkey bars, but much more painful because my hands and the backs of my knees were gripping splintery wood instead of smooth metal. Grunting with the effort, I pushed the rest of my lower body through the hole and rolled over so my stomach and hands supported me on the edge of the board. With both legs out it was easy to slide the rest of myself through and jump to the ground. *I did it!* I was actually standing outside.

After the semidarkness of the cabin, I was practically blind in the blazing sun, but my eyes adjusted quickly. My heart was pounding so hard it was a wonder the dogs couldn't hear it. Now all I had to do was run the hundred yards or so to the trees without anyone seeing me, and I'd be home free. No problem, as Iskinder would say. No problem at all.

Not wanting to waste a second, I started running as fast as I could, but I hadn't gone more than fifty feet when the dogs started barking again. How had they heard me running through the grass when they had slept through the giant thud of my knee hitting the wall? *Don't look back; just keep running.* And I did keep running, but it wasn't long before I heard voices shouting my name, "Stop! Lucy! Get back here!"

I ran even faster, ignoring the stitch I already had in my side. The tall grass was prickly and so thick it hid the rocks that were buried underneath, but I didn't have time to think about how much it hurt each time one of my bare feet landed on a stone. The trees weren't far now, but I could hear the barking dogs gaining on me, and I knew Markos, Helena, and Dawit were close behind. I dug three fingers under my rib cage to stop the pain and kept going.

Faster, faster.

Finally I reached the trees, but I couldn't slow down yet. There was no way I could outrun those dogs. I needed to find a place to hide. My senses zoomed in on every detail: the sudden drop in temperature, the dappled light, the twigs snapping under my feet, the gnarled bark on the trees, the faint scent of eucalyptus. I glanced up—that was where I needed to go. I would hide in the trees.

I ran wildly, directionless, searching for a tree I could climb. The dogs were still barking. *Tune them*

out, Lucy. Don't listen. There! I spotted a rock about the size of a small SUV next to a baobab tree with a long, low-enough-to-grab branch that was sticking straight out. I did a quick mental analysis: no thorns, good leaf coverage, sturdy-looking upper branches, and a clear climbing path to the canopy. An instant later I scrambled up the rock and leaped, catching the low branch in both hands. *Easy does it; it's just like the uneven bars.* I swung out, pushed myself up onto the branch, and started climbing. Gasping for breath, I climbed as high as I could until I reached the dense foliage about fifteen feet above the ground.

Eyes closed, I leaned my back against the tree trunk and braced my hands on the thick branch between my legs. I could hear Helena and Dawit calling for me, and when I glanced down, there was Markos standing directly under my tree while the two dogs sniffed the ground around him. *Don't look up; please, don't look up.* I held my breath and squeezed myself into the smallest, tightest ball I could.

And that's when I realized I wasn't alone.

Chapter Fourteen

Peering over my kneecaps, I looked straight into the small, round, black eyes of a colobus monkey.

She sat on a branch maybe ten feet above me (I guessed she was a she by her size—like a really big cat with a long white tail, super fluffy on the end like a feather duster), clutching a fistful of leaves and staring down at me as if I were some species of large, furless monkey she'd never seen before. Her silky black-and-white coat made her look like an overgrown tree skunk. Usually colobus monkeys are shy around people, but clearly she'd decided I wasn't a threat, which for some wacko reason made me feel slightly insulted: *Even a monkey can tell how scrawny and weak I am.*

I prayed she wouldn't make some hooty monkey noise and give me away. *That's right, Curious Georgina. Just keep eating your nice leaves, nice and quiet. . . .*

"Lucy!" Markos called. *Oh God, has he seen me?* "Where are you?" *No, he hasn't. Not yet, anyway.* "Come out, and we will take you to your parents." *Oh please, do you really think I'm going to fall for that, Mr. Psycho Dog-Killer?*

"You should not have run away, Lucy. We were just coming to tell you that we reached an agreement with your family," he cajoled, searching for me around the trees like the Child Catcher in *Chitty Chitty Bang Bang*. "Don't you want to go home? You cannot stay here; it is too dangerous. Come out, Lucy!" For a split second I almost believed him. I wanted to believe him so much, and he sounded so nice. Too nice. That's how I knew he was lying.

Markos stopped about ten feet away from my tree. He looked up, squinting against the sunlight that streamed though the trees, and I swear he stared right at me and Georgie. I froze, praying my green pants would help camouflage me among the leaves and that Georgie wouldn't pick now to have a screech festival. *Please, please, please, go away.*

When I opened my eyes again, he was gone—and so was Georgie. Which meant that for the first time in my entire life, I was really, totally alone.

No way, Lucy, don't go there. Not now. Okay, next topic. Something. Anything . . . monkeys.

Remembering that colobus monkeys always travel in groups, I scanned the trees near me. Sure enough, there they were, almost hidden by the shadows but visible if you concentrated. I counted twelve of them, including a snow-white baby clinging to her mother's belly. *How many more weeks until the fur starts to turn black?* I wondered.

I sat perfectly still, watching the monkeys. I decided the trees were like a primate spa, where the monkeys dined on healthy, all-natural foods, like leaves, bugs, and bark, and beautified each other, picking off pesky fleas and forest debris. A couple of them leaped away, swinging hand over hand through the trees until I couldn't see them anymore. Not for nothing are colobus monkeys considered the best climbers in Africa.

The monkeys seemed perfectly content, and why wouldn't they be? This was their home, their natural habitat, where they had everything they needed to do what monkeys do. All they had to worry about was avoiding predators. But me? Like the colobus, I had to worry about avoiding predators, including human predators. But unlike my primate cousins, I was way out of my element, with none of the things I needed to survive. Markos, Dawit, and Helena were bad enough. There were so many other ways I could die in this forest.

I could starve. *How long can a person go without food? Ten days? Two weeks?* To be fair, I knew that I would probably find something safe to eat before that happened, but you never know. After all, I had no idea how to tell if a plant was poisonous, and finding an animal that was willing to stand still long enough for me to kill it with my bare hands was kind of a long shot. I crossed my fingers and prayed for some nuts.

Dehydration was more likely than starvation. If I could find a water source—a stream, watering hole, anything—I'd be okay (forgetting the parasites for the moment). *If not, I'm hosed.*

Of course, all this foraging depended on my being able to forage. A sprained ankle could turn even

Tarzan into a sitting duck. Which brought me to my biggest fear of all—animals. A lion will kill you via suffocation. That's a nice way of saying tearing out your throat. Hyenas are even worse—they'll go straight for your guts. Even the cute animals like hippos and elephants are dangerous. Most people don't know this, but hippos and elephants can be extremely violent. If you get between a hippo and its water source, it'll rip the limbs right off your body with those big, powerful jaws. Elephants aren't very friendly either, especially if they've got babies around.

It was survival of the fittest, and let's face it, I wasn't very fit. I gave myself a day, two at the most. But I hoped it wouldn't come to that. I hoped I'd get lucky and find some kind of civilization before the day was out.

Which got me thinking. How would I know when it was safe to come down and start running again? It was nearly noon already—if I didn't leave soon, I might end up actually having to spend the night in the forest. A night. In the forest. Alone—with lions, hyenas, and snakes. *Oh my.*

• • •

It's funny how things change. Up until three days ago, spending a night in the forest seemed like nirvana. After Dahnie explained that nighttime was when all the action happened in the parks, I had begged Mom to let me stay out with him. This was before the Market Incident, so I actually thought there was a chance she'd say yes.

"How was the game drive?" she'd asked. She was sitting at her desk in the study.

"Amazing! Mom, you'll never believe it—we saw a whole pride of lions! Six of them—one male, two females, and three cubs. It was incredible!"

"Really?" Mom looked up from her work.

"Yeah, really. They were just lolling around, snoozing in the grass. Well, the cubs were playing, but the grown-ups were napping. Dahnie told me lions mostly sleep all day and if you want to see them in action, you have to come at night." I was winding up for my pitch.

"Is that so?"

I nodded. "That's what he told me. Dahnie sleeps out in the parks all the time. He says he just climbs a tree and he's perfectly safe."

"Well, I'm sure there are plenty of interesting things to see during the day too." *Ooh—ball one.* She went back to her paperwork.

I tried again. "Oh, of course there's stuff to see during the day. But the really interesting stuff happens at night. A lot of the wildlife here is nocturnal you know. Most of it is, actually."

"Uh-huh."

Was she even listening to me?

"Mom?"

"Yes, Luce?"

"Can I stay out with Dahnie in the park one night?"

Please say yes, please say yes, please say yes.

"Sure."

I couldn't believe it! "Really?"

Mom tossed her pen down on the desk with a big exhale. "Don't be ridiculous, Lucy. It's much too dangerous. Not to mention how it would look if you went camping overnight with an adult male park ranger."

"But, Mom," I pleaded, "we wouldn't have to be alone. We'll bring some marines. Nothing could possibly happen to me with Dahnie and two armed marines!"

"Oh, really? Remember what happened to the French ambassador's wife in Botswana? And she was with a whole touring party!"

I did remember. The French ambassador's wife had been flattened. By a hippo. Ugh.

"I'm sorry, Lucy," she said. "I know how much you want to do this, but I just can't—"

"You never let me do anything!" I screamed. I ran up to my room and slammed the door.

Five minutes later, there was a knock on the door. "Lucy," Mom said, "may I come in?"

I ignored her.

"Lucy?"

"Whatever," I said at last.

Mom came over and sat down on the bed next to me. I had my arms crossed in front of my chest and refused to look at her.

"I know it's hard for you here," she began. "I know there are a lot of things you want to do that you can't do, and there are a lot of things you don't want to do that you have to do." She put her hand on my knee, and I jerked it away. "And it doesn't help that I'm working all the time and that Daddy isn't with us."

You can say that again. I stared out the window so she wouldn't see the angry tears in my eyes.

"It won't always be this way," she said.

"Sure," I whispered.

She was quiet for a minute. "You know, Lucy, this job is very important to me."

Yeah, more important than I am. I was just amazed by the incredible hypocrisy of my mother, who devotes her entire life to "saving the world" but couldn't care less about her own child.

"It was a big opportunity, and it's turned out to be even more difficult than I'd expected. Every negotiation is a battle; no one is willing to compromise. . . ."

I can't believe her. Does she really expect my sympathy?

"Come on, Lucy, is it really so terrible living here in this beautiful house and going on game drives every week?"

Every other week, but who's counting? And what am I supposed to do during the other 332 hours? I gave her a disgusted look. She just didn't get it. The game drives were the only good thing in my life, and they were just a few short hours a couple of times a month. I hated being cooped up in the house all the time, reading about the world instead of living in it.

After waiting a while for me to say something, Mom finally gave up and left.

I was furious. How could she say she knows how bad things are and not do anything about it? *"A big opportunity," "so difficult," "very important."* When was she going to think about someone other than herself? I decided I couldn't—and wouldn't—take it any more. I called Dad at the office, and his secretary, Margaret, put me through right away, like always.

"Lulu!" I could picture him at his desk with that picture of me from first grade next to his computer, where he's always kept it. It was late afternoon in Jakarta, so his hair would be sticking out everywhere from running his hands through it all day, and his tie would be off. A half-eaten sandwich from lunch was probably still on his desk. My dad is kind of a slob. It was so good to hear his voice that I started crying.

"Sweetheart, what's the matter?"

"It's Mom," I sobbed.

"Mom?" he sounded alarmed. "Is everything all right?"

"No, it's nothing like that. It's . . . it's . . ."

Finally, I got the words out. "I hate it here! All I do is sit around the house and go to a stupid school and stupid dinners with stupid boring people. And Mom knows! She knows it's awful, and she knows I hate it, and she doesn't care. All she cares about is her job." I took a deep breath. "I want to come live with you."

"Oh, Lulu, I'm sorry."

"She's not!" I shot back.

"First of all, your mother is not 'she.' And second of all, Mom loves you and cares about you very much."

"Well, she's got a great way of showing it."

"Let me ask you something, Lucy. Why are you so angry with your mother?"

"I just told you," I said. "I have no life, and it's her fault!"

"So you say. But why aren't you mad at me?"

I hadn't thought of that before. Why wasn't I mad at him? After all, they made all their decisions together. "Because you're nice. Because you care."

"Mom cares, too, Lucy. Look, when we decided Mom would take this ambassadorship, we both thought it would be a great chance for you to experience a new culture. It's true, we didn't anticipate how much Mom would be working, but you're old enough to appreciate that this job is a very big deal for her. It's a huge honor and a big step up in her career. I don't think your life is so terrible that you can't make the best of it."

I was stunned. I had expected him to take my side, and instead he'd made me feel like a selfish brat. Indignant rage had felt so much better.

"Lucy?"

"Fine," I said grimly. "I'll make the best of it."

• • •

But I didn't try to make the best of it, did I? Just as Mom never tried to see things from my point of view, I never tried to see them from hers. And where had it gotten me? Up a tree. Literally.

Chapter Fifteen

My rear end was sore from sitting on a branch for so long, and my back was killing me where a knot in the trunk had dug into my skin. These new afflictions, along with all my other aches and pains, meant that just two hours into my escape, my already-minuscule odds of survival were sinking even lower. I hadn't heard Markos, Dawit, Helena, or the dogs for more than half an hour, but I was terrified that the minute I climbed out of the tree, they'd show up. I also knew I had to get moving. The question was, Where? How was I going to find other people?

Water.

Teddy had once explained that because there's

almost no plumbing outside the major cities, villages have to be near a natural water source. So if I could find water, maybe I would find people.

I tried to remember what Dahnie had said about finding signs that water was near. *Follow animal tracks.* Well, so far I hadn't seen any animal tracks . . . but I had seen animals, hadn't I? The colobus monkeys had all leaped away in the same direction. Maybe they were on their way to find water.

I felt a flicker of hope that was almost big enough to call excitement. *Maybe I can actually do this.*

I scrambled down the tree as fast as I could. It was easy until I reached that horizontal branch. There was no way to jump back onto the rock without breaking my neck, so I hung from the branch and dropped to the ground about six feet below.

Damn it! I landed right on the sharp end of a broken tree branch. I could tell from the pain that it was bad. Fighting back tears, I sat down to inspect my foot. Sure enough, there was a big gash in the arch, near the ball of my foot. Blood flowed pretty freely—it wasn't gushing, but it was more than just a bad scrape. Feeling utterly hopeless, I sat there slumped over with my face in my hands. *I can't do this. I'm an idiot. Can't, can't, can't do it.*

Except I had to. There was no turning back now. Furiously, I pulled off my T-shirt and tore a hole in it with my teeth. Then I ripped the bottom four inches off in one long strip. Ignoring how filthy it was, I wrapped the cloth tightly around my foot and knotted it, hoping the pressure would stop the bleeding. I put my shirt back on—luckily there was still enough left to cover me.

Standing was okay, but walking hurt like crazy. I spotted a long, strong branch on the ground and pulled off the little twiggy parts so I could use it as a walking stick. Then I checked my compass and began limping northeast.

And here's the crazy thing: The forest was beautiful. More than beautiful—it was peaceful and quiet, as if nothing had disturbed it in a million years. There must have been animals around, but they were all hidden in the brush. If it weren't for the chorus of birds squawking and chirping, I would swear I had the whole place to myself. The trees made a lush canopy overhead, protecting my skin from the sun and my body from the worst of the heat. I thought I could smell fruit trees, and my mouth started to water like Pavlov's dog.

I was starving, but there was no time for a mango hunt. Instead, I let myself eat a small piece of the *injera* while I walked. I felt like Gretel, desperately trying to escape the clutches of the evil witch and find her way home. What would she have done without Hansel? Nobody can survive alone. Come to think of it, Jane Goodall had brought her mother with her to Africa; Biruté Galdikas had brought her husband to Borneo. And Dian Fossey went alone and got kidnapped. *Gee, there's a lesson in there somewhere.*

I knew I had better find water soon because I was so thirsty I was sure I was about to start hallucinating. And even though I had just eaten, my stomach was killing me. I paused for what Americans call a bathroom break and the Ethiopians call a bush stop.

It seemed the parasites had finally made themselves at home. Between the heat and my new digestion problems, dehydration was probably minutes away—if I wasn't dehydrated already.

The monkeys were nowhere to be found, but I had

noticed that a lot of the birds seemed to be flying in the same direction that I was walking. I crossed my fingers and continued northeast.

I kept my head down as I walked, looking for tracks, even as I kept my ears open, listening for Markos and the others. The ground was uneven, with lots of hidden rocks and scrubby brush. If I got hungry enough, would I be willing to turn over one of those rocks and eat whatever happened to be crawling underneath?

I turned a corner around a pretty sizable boulder and spotted what could have been animal tracks in the earth: oval-shaped indentations that could have been made by the hooves of some deerlike creature. I kept walking, and there were more. Now I was pretty sure they must be tracks. I picked up my pace even though my foot was killing me. Just the possibility of a drink—not to mention being able to wash my cut—made the pain bearable.

The tracks led back through some trees, and before too much longer, there it was: a stream! My very own stream that I had found all by myself. It was trickly and meager, and maybe it was raging with parasites, but I didn't care—it was wet. I leaned down and began scooping mouthfuls of water as fast as I could. It was warm and muddy and tasted like clay, but has anything ever been sweeter? I actually laughed as I drank, I was so relieved. Finding this stream felt like the biggest accomplishment of my entire life.

After I finished drinking, I carefully unwrapped my foot and inspected the damage. Thankfully, it didn't look infected—yet. I dabbed my foot in the water and used my hand and the bandage to clean the cut as best I could, grinding my teeth against the sting. Then I swished the bandage around in the stream and rubbed it against a rock to get as much dirt out as possible. When I was finished, my foot actually looked clean and the bandage looked a bit better too. I wrung the extra water out of the bandage and let my foot air-dry before wrapping it up again.

Now that I had found my stream, I was never going to leave it. My stream, I decided, was my salvation. It would give me water; it would lead me back to civilization. I named it Moses.

Okay, Mo. Whither thou goest, I too shall go. Isn't that in the Bible somewhere? I walked along the edge of the stream, listening to the birds calling and the occasional scurrying noise of some small animal I couldn't see. Luckily, there were no signs of Markos, Helena, or Dawit. Had they given up? Doubtful—it had only been a few hours. A few of the bushes had small red berries, but hungry as I was, I was too scared to eat them. A couple bites of *injera* would have to do. If I could forget about the awful reason for this walkabout, I could actually see enjoying myself. Exploring the African bush on my own had been a lifelong fantasy. I was Mowgli in *Jungle Book,* Tarzan, king of the apes (or in my case, of the colobus), and of course Lucy in Narnia.

But I couldn't forget. My progress was slow because of my foot, and as the afternoon wore on and there were still no signs of civilization, I got more and more worried. Finally I had to face reality: I was actually going to have to spend the night alone in the bush. I stopped short and hugged myself tightly, trying not to cry. *Deep breaths, Lucy. Think.* Staying on the ground would be suicide, I knew. I looked up at the trees. Okay, which one of you would be home for tonight?

It had to be easy to climb and with enough leaves on top to screen me from any nighttime predators. A big, thick comfy (comfy!) branch was essential, and I didn't want to be too close to Moses, since animals would be likely to use the stream as a water source during the night—like the lions I had been hearing or, God forbid, hyenas.

There are a lot of hyenas in Ethiopia. At night they prowl in packs, their shaggy brown spotted fur matted with dirt, reeking of the blood from their most recent kill or of the "hyena butter" they secrete from their butts to mark their territories (how gross is that?). Their massive jaws are the strongest in the animal kingdom. Hyenas are the only animals I know of whose young kill each other—besides humans, that is.

I don't know why hyenas are called "laughing." "Laughing" suggests something happy, like a good joke or a child playing on the beach. The hyena's bark sounds more like an evil witch's cackle. It's no wonder hyenas are to Africans what black cats are to Westerners. There's even a mythical were-hyena here—like a werewolf except that the man's killer alter ego is a hyena instead of a wolf.

Finally I found it: the perfect tree, with lots of leaves and big branches that wouldn't be too hard to climb. It was a sycamore—the African kind, not the kind we have at home. Dahnie had told me the Egyptians called the sycamore the tree of life, which I decided was a good sign. I looked up and scanned the branches: no pythons. Next to the sycamore was an acacia, which I considered longingly. But the two-inch thorns covering every branch made the umbrella tree an impossible choice. Like a lion, my favorite tree is beautiful but dangerous.

It was getting dark, but before climbing up, I stopped for one last drink and bush stop. If I needed to go during the night, I would just have to hang my butt off the branch like a monkey. *Can my life get any weirder?*

Hands on the trunk of the sycamore, I paused, irresistibly drawn to the thorny umbrella tree. I craved the safe and peaceful feeling the acacias gave me out in the bush. I thought if I could just sit under the acacia for a little while, maybe I wouldn't feel so scared and alone. Just a couple of minutes wouldn't be too dangerous, would it? Only five minutes, I promised myself, not a second more, and I'd keep my eyes peeled and my ears open the whole time.

I sat down slowly, leaned my back against the trunk, and felt my tight muscles relax. It felt so good to rest and to pretend I was anywhere but here. *I'm not in Africa, not alone. I'm home, under a tree. It's Christmas.*

.   .   .

Christmas is my favorite holiday, and my favorite Christmas was when I was eight years old. It was back before my mother had started working so hard, before everything changed. We were in Maryland for the holidays, and we were making our annual trip up to Philadelphia to spend the day with Mom's cousins, the ones Dad calls the Dreary Dunlops. Not that their last name is Dunlop. Dad does that with everyone; it's part of his strange sense of humor. I'm Lulu (after another opera heroine—this one gets murdered by Jack the Ripper), Mom's sister, Victoria, is Naughty Nora, and Grandma Catherine is the Battle-Ax.

Anyway, after acknowledging Dad's Jewish heritage with a breakfast of bagels and lox, we crammed the car with everyone's presents and set off.

Mom and Dad starting fighting almost as soon as we pulled out of the driveway.

"It's not as if we see them all the time, Dan. Is

it so terrible that I want to be with my family on Christmas?"

"Willa, you're not *listening* to me. Of course you should see your family on Christmas. But does it have to be the same thing, the same people, every year?"

"It's called tradition! Ever hear of it?"

I hated it when they fought. "Can you please have this argument some other time?"

"No!" they shouted in unison.

"All married couples argue, Lucy," my father said in his most sincere fatherly tone. "It doesn't mean Mom and I don't love each other."

I was beginning to feel nauseated, and I didn't think it was just from listening to my parents.

"I feel sick."

"You don't feel sick," Mom said. "You just don't want us to argue."

"No, I really feel sick."

"Why don't you lean back and try to have a nap, Lulu?" Dad suggested.

I closed my eyes and tried to tune out their whispered bickering, which got louder and louder every minute.

 143

"Mom?"

"What!"

"I really think I'm going to be sick. Daddy, pull over!"

But it was too late. By the time Dad got the car to the shoulder, I had already vomited smoked salmon and cream cheese all over the new car—and Mom.

My parents looked at each other.

"No problem!" Dad exclaimed brightly. "We'll just do Christmas at our house!"

Half an hour later, there I was, tucked into my parents' bed, clean and cozy in my favorite blue flannel nightgown. My stomach felt a lot better, and Mom had brought me a tray of ginger ale and saltines.

"Ho-ho-ho!" sang Dad. He and Mom stood smiling in the doorway, wearing matching Santa hats and carrying shopping bags of presents.

They sat on the bed with me, and together we opened our gifts. I don't remember them all, but I do remember Dad gave Mom antique garnet earrings and a matching bracelet, and Mom gave Dad a beautiful hourglass. I got a CD player, some books (of course), and best of all, a real fossilized saber-toothed tiger fang that was more than 500,000 years old.

"Why don't you try to take a nap, sweetie?" said Mom at last. She was rubbing my back in big, slow circles.

I rolled over, and they both leaned in to kiss me at the same time, one on each cheek. A Lucy sandwich.

After they left, I played with Dad's hourglass for a while. The afternoon sun sparkled against the green and blue glass. I watched the sand stream through the narrow opening and pile into a dune in the bottom bulb until I drifted off to sleep, barely aware of the sound of my parents' laughter coming from the next room.

. . .

My parents' laughter? No! Those were *hyenas*—hyenas somewhere close!

Chapter Sixteen

Night Three

Instantly wide awake, I sprang to my feet and stared saucer-eyed into the black night. I practically flew the ten feet to the sycamore and scrambled up the trunk as fast as I could. My heart pounded in my chest, and I couldn't catch my breath. Hyenas! I had visions of my guts spilling out and my blood pumping into the dirt. I couldn't bear to think about it.

I wrapped both arms around the tree trunk and pressed my cheek against the reassuring solidity of its rough bark, hardly aware of the throbbing in my foot. *I'm okay, I'm okay.* Slowly I counted *one Mississippi, two Mississippi, three Mississippi,* until my breathing returned to normal. At two-hundred-four Mississippi, I noticed my stomach growling and gurgling—though whether from hunger or parasites or both was impossible to tell. I ate the last of my *injera* and tried not to think about life alone in the wilds of Ethiopia with no food. The setting of the sun had taken the edge off the intense heat, although not enough to stop the sweat trickling down my neck and back. But, I reasoned, as long as I was sweating, I couldn't be too dehydrated. At least I had one thing to be grateful for.

I forced myself to keep thinking about all of my physical problems to take my mind off the hyenas that continued to squeal and cackle nearby. I could picture them clearly: their batlike faces, bushy spotted fur, and bizarre sloping haunches. After all, this wasn't my first hyena encounter.

. . .

Right after we'd arrived in Ethiopia, back when I was still allowed out of the house (well, at least every now and then), my mother had taken a meet-and-greet trip to the city of Harar and had brought me along. Harar is all the way east in Ethiopia, less than a hundred miles from the Somalian border. With about ninety mosques in just one square kilometer, it's famous for being one of the most important Muslim cities in the world. It's also famous for its hyena man.

Inside the city walls, ancient whitewashed buildings, some painted now-faded blues, greens, and reds, alternated with corrugated-tin-roofed houses along dirt roads. Crowding the roads are horse and cart taxis for people lucky enough to be able to pay for them and men in turbans and long robes leading camels loaded with firewood. While my mother droned on in endless dull conversation with Harari officials, I had plenty of opportunity to study the tall women in their tie-dyed dresses, bright underskirts, and saffron head scarves. Some of them carried huge baskets on their heads, and I couldn't figure out how they managed to stay upright, walking on the uneven roads under all that weight. A few had babies on their backs nearly hidden under filmy scarves.

Naturally, we traveled in an entourage, and anything too dirty or the tiniest bit unpleasant was whisked away before it could lessen our enjoyment or positive impression of the local attractions. Everywhere we went, people cried out *"Ferenji! Ferenji!"* Foreigner! Foreigner! I heard it so often I felt like one of those one-named celebrities: *Ferenji, Live in Concert!* I felt rich, white, and conspicuous.

"Such a wonderful new road you've built between Dire Dawa and Harar, Mr. Garane," my mother commented to one of the officials.

"Thank you, Madam Ambassador. Chinese construction companies built the road. They are also building the new water pipe that will bring water along the same route."

I tuned them out, instead watching a small boy throw scraps of meat from the butcher's market to the kite birds that lurked nearby. Each time he tossed a piece into the air, the birds swarmed the sky, diving for their prey. The boy couldn't have been more than six or seven, but he was clearly out on his own, with no mother in sight. *If only we could trade places.*

We passed a narrow street lined with men sitting at sewing machines. "What's that?" I asked Hassan, our guide.

"The street is called Makina Gir Gir," he explained, "for the sound the sewing machines make. The men, they are all tailors. Many people buy clothes from them."

"Cool! Can we walk that way?"

"It is not on our route," the other official said quickly.

It seemed like there were a lot of things that weren't on our route. We walked *past* the smugglers' market, *past* Selassie's dilapidated birthplace, where an old medicine man now lives, *past* the blacksmith, *past* just about everything I would have wanted to see.

At last, we were back at our car. Mr. Garane clapped his hands together and said, "And so, I hope you have enjoyed seeing our city! Madam Ambassador, you and Lucy will join us at seven for dinner, yes?"

"Yes, seven—"

"Mom!" I interrupted. "I thought we were going to see the hyena man tonight!" The hyena man was going to be the only fun part of the trip.

"There's been a change of plans, Lucy," my mother explained with a look that said, *Not now.*

I couldn't believe it—she had promised me we would go.

Hassan cleared his throat. "Madam Ambassador, maybe I can take Lucy to see the hyena man tonight?" he offered.

"Yeah!" I said.

"No," said my mother at the same time.

"Thank you, Hassan," said my mother with a polite nod, "but Lucy is coming to dinner with me." I gave her a look that I hoped resembled a drowning man, which she ignored.

"Mom!" I started, but she grabbed me by the elbow before I could say anything more.

"Excuse us, everyone," she said to Hassan and the officials, dragging me halfway down the street.

"Don't you *ever* contradict me in front of other adults! Especially when I'm working."

It was the cardinal rule, and I had broken it. *Too bad.* "I'm sorry, Mom, but you're taking away the one thing I was excited about doing!"

"I know, Lucy, but this dinner is important."

"Why do I have to be there?"

"Because I just don't feel comfortable about you going to see the hyenas without me. They're wild animals. Do you know how this hyena man got his job? The last one got his left hand bitten off!"

"So you're saying I have to give up a once-in-a-lifetime opportunity so you can drag me to yet another boring business dinner?"

"I'm sorry if you think it's boring, but that's the way it has to be."

But I wasn't going to give up so easily. I switched strategies. "Look, Mom, the people at the dinner don't care about me—you know that. I swear I won't go near the hyenas. And I can go with a marine, too. Come on, Mom, you're the one who joined the Peace Corps and went traveling around Africa *alone* for three years! Can't I have a little excitement too?"

"That was different. For one thing, I was an adult," she paused, clearly wrestling with herself. Despite her obsessive all-business exterior, I knew that somewhere buried way down deep inside my mother beat the heart of an adventurer. After all, it wasn't so many years ago that my mother had been that adventurer.

"Please, Mom? It would mean so much to me."

My mother sighed. "Okay, okay, you can go."

I beamed.

"But promise me you'll be careful," she added, pulling my head toward her and giving me a kiss on my forehead.

"I promise."

Shortly after nightfall, there we were: me, Hassan, and Kevin, the world's largest marine, gathered in a dirt clearing outside the city walls with Yousef the hyena man. A small man with hair like fuzzy gray wool and deeply wrinkled dark skin (and two hands), he sat in the dirt with a basket of bloody bits of meat, the butcher's leftovers, at his feet. The full moon and the headlights from our car gave off the only light.

Hassan explained that the people of Harar believe that if they feed the hyenas that live near the city and prowl the streets at night, the hyenas will leave them in peace. Then Yousef spoke to us in Harari, and Hassan translated: "You must be fearless. If you have no fear, the hyenas will respect you and will not harm you. Watch. You will see."

Yousef grinned and held up the basket. I practically gagged when I saw that his hands were slick and shiny with animal guts. Then he tipped back his head and began to call out something that sounded like "*Ma-ooooor-ab! Ya!*"

"The hyena man gives them names," Hassan explained. "Here comes Black Tail; that one is named

Hungry"—*did he say HUNGRY???*—"over there is Long Nose."

I staggered back as eight sets of bright eyes like glowing mirrors emerged from the darkness. We held our breath and stared as, not ten feet from us, Yousef began to feed the hyenas, taking chunks of meat and bones from his basket and offering them to the animals. One by one they approached him in what was clearly a familiar routine, tearing the meat from the end of a stick, from his hand, and then—I couldn't believe it—straight from Yousef's mouth.

Yousef looked them right in the eye the whole time and never stopped speaking to them in a calm, soothing voice. It seemed to me that there was some kind of connection between the hyena man and his hyenas. He gave them food, and they gave him—what? Not power—it didn't look to me as if he had any kind of power over them—but maybe respect, like he said. Or maybe not. Maybe so far Yousef had been just plain lucky.

Yousef looked up at us and gestured. "Do you want to try?" asked Hassan.

"Yes!" I said instantly, even though the prospect terrified me.

But Kevin put his giant hand firmly on my shoulder. "Sorry, Lucy."

For once I didn't argue. Yousef may have felt he had nothing to fear, but these were definitely not pets; they were wild animals. And they were ferocious. The hyenas snatched the meat, grunting and violently chewing and tearing until not a morsel was left. Then they paced around, jerking their heads from side to side to see if any more food was coming before Yousef waved his hand and sent them back into the darkness.

. . .

I didn't know how I would survive the night up in a tree. Even though I was completely exhausted, I was too terrified to sleep. I was scared I'd fall off my branch, that my kidnappers would find me, that any of at least a dozen creatures would come slithering and creeping my way—beetles, biting ants, giant flying cockroaches, chiggers, pythons, leopards, monkeys. I could picture them all, sneaking up on me one by one to claim their fair share of my already bite-covered flesh. I was being morbid, I knew, but who wouldn't be in my situation? I kept thinking about Dahnie: *"Just sleep in a tree. It's what we all do!"* Yeah, Dahnie, easy for you to say, with your thick hiking boots and your big rifle.

The trees blocked out whatever moonlight or starlight there might have been, and the total darkness made my fears ten times worse. I could make out my hand in front of my face but not much more. Somehow the dark amplified all the forest noises, and each crackle and hoot triggered a jolt of adrenaline. After a couple of hours I was so wired, my hands were shaking.

The hyenas cackled on and off all night, and twice I heard the thunderous roars of those lions. It was incredible. The power of that sound made the whole forest stand still. A few times I thought I could detect noises near Moses, probably some nocturnal animals stopping by for a nightcap. I prayed they wouldn't smell me. Although after three days in this heat without a shower, I had to imagine that smelling me wouldn't be too difficult.

But bad as it was up in the tree, I was more scared

of going down in the morning. How would I stay ahead of Markos, Dawit, and Helena while limping around on this stupid foot? I knew they wouldn't give up the search so easily. And how was I ever going to find someone, anyone, to help me? I had assumed Moses would lead me to some kind of village, since people tend to settle near water. But how long would that take, and could I hold out? And what if I was wrong? Between my foot, my stomach, and my lack of food, my prospects looked pretty bleak.

I tried not to think about what was happening, about *them,* but no matter how hard I tried, I couldn't get rid of the dull ache in my chest or the ice in my fingertips—the feeling of panic that threatened to erupt from my stomach like a geyser and spew from my mouth in an endless, wailing shriek: *Noooooooooo!!!* I'm pretty sure I didn't sleep a single minute all night, but at some point my nerves gave out and numbness replaced terror, which was a definite improvement.

Dad always said things looked better in the morning, and usually he was right.

I just hope I'll make it until morning.

Chapter Seventeen

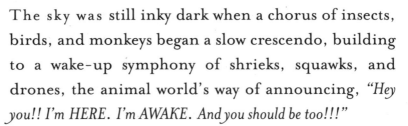

Day Four

The sky was still inky dark when a chorus of insects, birds, and monkeys began a slow crescendo, building to a wake-up symphony of shrieks, squawks, and drones, the animal world's way of announcing, *"Hey you!! I'm HERE. I'm AWAKE. And you should be too!!!"*

When dawn finally arrived, the noise died down some, and to my relief Dad's cliché proved to be true: For no reason at all, things did look better. I watched the color seep back into the trees and felt calm. The air smelled sweet, and the early light played against the heart-shaped leaves and the nuts that hung among them.

The *nuts*?

I stood up on my branch and held the trunk for balance, trying to get a closer look at the round brown objects hanging not far from my head.

They weren't nuts. They were *figs*. Figs! I laughed out loud. Here I'd spent the whole night practically dying of starvation when there had been food hanging all around me! I grabbed five and ate them in seconds, splitting the peel and scooping out the red and green flesh with my teeth. Figs probably weren't the best food choice for my poor stomach, but they were the only choice, and after days of nothing but *injera*, they tasted more delicious than chocolate soufflé, strawberry ice cream, and Grandma Catherine's rice pudding all rolled into one. I ate until I was full and then stuffed my pockets with as many figs as I could cram in.

I was exhausted and my circumstances hadn't changed, but at least my belly was full. I climbed down carefully and retrieved my walking stick from the ground under the acacia, where I'd left it. I was ready to face whatever the day would bring.

Moses was deserted. I rinsed my wound and the bandage and was relieved to see there were still no signs of infection. I even broke a small twig and used the frayed end to brush my teeth the way I'd seen some African kids do it. A long drink topped off my fig breakfast, and after a giant stretch I was off, limping after Moses wherever he chose to go.

It was still early, so the sun wasn't too strong. I figured this was probably going to be the nicest part of the day and I should enjoy it as much as possible. As I walked, I sang song after song in my head, curious to see how long I could go before I ran out of new ones.

There were no signs of you-know-who, and I was feeling pretty good, all things considered. A beautiful red and orange kingfisher caught my eye, but I didn't stop to admire it. I needed to get to wherever I was going as fast as I could. Up ahead I could see Moses flowing out of the trees and into a clearing. I noted that he was getting bigger and wondered whether he would turn into a watering hole. Sure enough, just beyond the tree line I could see what looked like a small pond. Stepping out from the trees, I was just about to drop to my knees, grateful for a drink of water that didn't have mud visibly swirling around in it, when out of the corner of my eye I saw something twitch. I froze. The hairs on the back of my neck stood up, and goose bumps popped up all over my arms.

There, twenty feet straight ahead and on the same side of the water as me, stood three grown lions. A male and two females. I had interrupted them while they were drinking. Water dripped from their chins, along with some blood from a recent kill.

For an eternity nothing moved. We just stared at each other. Gradually, I became aware of a whimpering sound, and I wondered if the animal they had just eaten might still be alive nearby. Then I realized the whimpering sound was me.

The lion raised his massive head and looked straight into my eyes and through me. His black mane was short, and I could see spots on his nose—he was young. One of the females sat down and began cleaning her face with a paw, just like a house cat only much, much bigger. The other one went back to drinking. All that separated us was a few feet of grass, like a corridor that ran between the pond on my left side and the trees on my right. Beyond them the stream continued into an open field.

"Anbasa," I whispered.

They ignored me, totally indifferent to my presence. But I couldn't take my eyes off them. The bushy tufts at the ends of their tales, their pale swollen bellies marked by faint spots, their big, round paws, claws retracted for now but there nonetheless, inches long and lethal. The weird thing was, I didn't feel afraid. I felt *electrified*.

Suddenly there was a loud rustling from the trees, and I whipped my head around to see what was coming. I heard their voices before I saw them: Markos, Dawit, and Helena. The dogs must have followed my scent. It couldn't have been too hard, especially with a fresh cut on my foot.

Markos, Dawit, and Helena jerked to a stop as soon as they saw the lions, their expressions ranging from shock to terror. The dogs strained against their leashes back toward the trees, desperate to get away from the predators. We stood in a triangle, with me at one corner, the lions straight ahead, and Markos, Helena, and Dawit to my right, near the trees. One lioness flicked her tail, a sign of annoyance. I wanted to tell her, *It's their fault I'm here—blame them, not me!!*

Markos was the first to recover. "You stupid, stupid

girl." His quiet voice seethed with anger. "Look at what you have done."

Dawit held up his hand. "Enough, Markos," he murmured. "Lucy. Back up very slowly and make your way to us. It will be okay. Move very slowly, and do not show the lions your back."

But I had no intention of moving. I had made my choice two nights ago when I decided to escape.

"Lucy," urged Helena, "you can't stay here. The lions will kill you. Please—"

"And do you know how they will kill you?" Markos interrupted. "First, they will tear out your throat. Next, they will rip open your stomach with their claws. If you are lucky, you will be dead before that happens."

His words wiped out any doubt I might have felt. "And what about you, Markos?" I said, keeping my voice low but strong and even. "How will you kill me? Do tell me, please. I want to make an informed choice."

That did it. Markos started toward me, but before he took two steps, the lion stood up.

The lion stood up.

The lion walked slowly, deliberately, directly toward me, and the lionesses followed him. The king of the jungle and his two queens were ten feet away. Nine. Eight. Five.

None.

Three gigantic beasts surrounded me, their heads almost level with mine. I couldn't move, couldn't breathe. Silent tears poured down my cheeks. It was like my body was experiencing what was happening while my brain was observing everything from a distance. Mesmerized, I watched the lions' rib cages expand and contract with each heavy breath. The male leaned forward.

I'm going to die.

But with one long stride he turned to face the other humans. Helena and Dawit staggered back, wide-eyed and openmouthed. Markos wasn't intimidated so easily. Of course not. He was the one with the gun, which he was gripping so hard I could see the tendons in his hands.

The standoff was broken by a low, rumbling growl from one of the lionesses. Then the lion tossed his head and stretched his mouth into a wide grimace, bearing every one of his two-inch-long teeth. Markos flinched. He had about ten seconds to get of there, and he knew it.

"You had your chance, Lucy," he called as he backed away. "Move," he ordered the others.

Helena's shoulders were shaking with quiet sobs as they fell back into the trees. Dawit was the last to go. Just before he disappeared, he said, "I am sorry, Lucy." *Yeah, thanks for nothing.*

My head swam as the enormity of it hit me: I was safe from my kidnappers—but surrounded by wild lions.

I let out a small moan, and with it went all of my courage. My shaky legs couldn't support me anymore. I sank down into the grass and hid my face in my hands, too scared to see what would happen next.

To my utter amazement, what happened next turned out to be—nothing. With the big humans gone, the lions went back to ignoring me and ambled over to a particularly shady tree and lay down. *Now what?* I was trapped. I couldn't go back, I couldn't follow Markos, Dawit, and Helena into the trees, and the lions blocked Moses's path ahead of me. How much time did I have left until they got hungry again? I sat where I was in the increasingly hot sun and sneaked glances at them out of the corner of my eye while they dozed.

I fantasized about living among the lions out in the wild. They would hunt, and I would build a fire and roast the leftovers for myself. During the day we'd sleep together in one big cozy heap, and at night we'd go exploring. Sometimes the lion would even let me ride on his back. I would be Lady Lucy of the Lions, and the stories about me would live on forever as legends of bravery and adventure.

One of the lionesses was still awake, studying me as I studied her. I stared into her amber eyes, so calm and unknowable, and wondered what she saw in me. We stayed like that for a long time, communing. Like Yousef and his hyenas.

You must not be afraid. Show them respect.

You must not be afraid.

What did I have to lose?

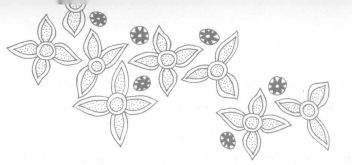

Chapter Eighteen

Slowly, without breaking eye contact with the lioness, I got to my feet. I took two deep breaths, drew back my shoulders, and set my face in what I hoped was a peaceful, confident, but unchallenging expression.

I took a step forward. The lioness raised her head but stayed where she was. The other two kept sleeping. *So far, so good. Just take it one step at a time.* And I did. Step by step, I approached the lions, talking softly to them the whole time.

"Okay, friendly lions, I'm just going to walk by you now so I can keep going on that path over there. No problem, I'm just walking nice and slow; you can stay right where you are; I won't bother you. That's right, here I am, getting closer now, but it's okay; you just keep resting, and I'll keep walking."

I was just a few feet in front of them now, and they were all awake, watching me. I scanned their bodies, looking for any signs of anger or annoyance, a tense muscle, a yawn, a flick of a tail. But no, they just looked back at me the same way I was looking at them. Politely.

"Here we go, lions, I'm walking past you now, past you and then away, that's right."

I stared straight ahead as I walked, hands at my sides with the palms out so the lions could see them. To get around the lions, I had to pass within inches of the male, and when I did, I felt something graze my fingers. My heart leaped to my throat. Terrified, I looked down.

The lion was sniffing me.

"Oh!" I exclaimed softly, my whole body tingling. I resisted the overpowering urge to yank my hand away and stayed perfectly still while he made his way from my hand to my wrist. I inhaled his warm, doggy smell, and then slowly and gently I extended my fingers and touched his bristly fur. It reminded me of a German shepherd.

"Nice to meet you too," I whispered. It really felt that way. He just seemed to be—I don't know, *exploring.* Imagine that—a lion exploring me!

But I had to keep moving. "Thank you for saving my life," I whispered.

After I had walked about thirty feet, I risked looking back. But they were invisible, hidden by the tall grass that separated us. I could almost believe the whole thing had never happened except that my body still hummed with excitement and relief. It was a false sense of security, though. I knew that even after leaving me to be eaten alive by wild animals, Markos, Dawit, and Helena wouldn't give up without seeing my chewed up bones with their own eyes.

My buzzing nerves were completely at odds with the peacefulness of my new surroundings: an open field of dry grass dotted with scrub bushes, bunches of acacias, and here and there a massive ficus tree. The aqua sky stretched forever without any sign that a single human being had ever been under it—no rooftops or smoke or airplanes whizzing by. During the rainy season all of this was probably lush and flowery, but now, dried out by the relentless sun, it was mostly brown.

Which meant if I didn't do something soon, I was going to be fried. With my green eyes and beyond-pale freckled skin, I'm the last person who should have been spending extended periods of time outside in equatorial Africa. And unfortunately, I seemed to have forgotten my sunscreen.

Somehow I had to cover my skin. But what could I use? I looked around, and inspiration struck. Once again Moses came to my rescue. I scooped up handfuls of mud from his banks and smeared it over every exposed inch of my body and then some—face, neck, arms, legs, stomach, back, ears, eyelids, even up into my hairline. The cool mud felt so good I didn't even care what I looked like. My first thought was of one of those gnome pencils we used to collect in second grade, the ones that you rub back and forth between your hands to make the fluorescent hair stand out. I patted my head gingerly. My hair was stiff with days of sweat and filth and now a generous application of mud.

A flash of movement out in the field caught my eye and I snapped to attention. I spotted two—no, three—no, *more* antelope. A small herd ambled across the grassland and stopped to graze about twenty yards from me. They weren't very big, about five feet high. Some were chocolate brown and others were more yellowish—according to gender, I hypothesized. I looked carefully at their horns: They curved out, then forward, and then backward. And then it dawned on me—they weren't just any old antelope; they were hartebeest. *Swayne's* hartebeest! If I had had two good feet, I would have done a little dance, but as it was I did a finger boogie instead, shaking my shoulders and jabbing my index fingers at the sky. I knew where I was! *Wahoo!*

I love you, Swayne's hartebeest! I want to marry you! I want to be you! Has there ever been a more perfect, more beautiful, more brilliant antelope than a Swayne's hartebeest? How kind of you to be practically extinct and living only in four tiny regions of Ethiopia! And how much of a genius am I to have spent ten thousand million hours rereading Haines's Guide to African Mammals, *fifth edition, so that I could, in a flash of truly astonishing mental acuity, recognize you? Lions plus Swayne's hartebeest plus ficus trees plus sycamore figs plus savanna and woodland equal* Oromo Region near Lake Chamo*!*

And then a teeny, tiny mouse voice whispered in my ear, "Psst, Lucy, who else lives near Lake Chamo?"

It was too scary good to even think about, but it was true: *Teddy.* Guge, his village, is near Lake Chamo. But that did *not,* I reminded myself sternly, mean I was really near his village. *Near* means "within fifty miles." My foot would turn gangrenous and fall off before I walked fifty miles. But what if his village wasn't fifty miles away? What if it was just beyond that group of trees over there? It wouldn't be the first time Teddy had offered me a refuge in a hostile environment.

• • •

The first time was when we met, on my second day at the International School. I had noticed that not one single kid seemed to want to have anything to do with me, but I couldn't figure out why. After all, I had been the new kid so many times I was usually pretty good at fitting in.

I got lost on the way to English class that day, and when I finally got there, everyone was already sitting down. There were only three empty seats—all clustered around Teddy, who was sitting alone in the back corner of the room. I sat down next to him.

"Welcome to the leper colony," he whispered.

"Excuse me?" I whispered back.

"This section of the room is for the Untouchables, the lowest caste of International School society."

"Oh really? I didn't know I was a member of that caste," I told him, wondering, *Is this kid some kind of freak?*

"You have not heard? At this school the only thing worse than being poor is being American," he explained. "At least I am lucky enough not to be American," he added with just a hint of a smile. *I get it—he's not a freak; he's funny. This is good. I like funny.*

"Why don't people like Americans?" I asked, opening *Romeo and Juliet* to the beginning of Act II.

"Not all of the kids. Just the Europeans. But at this school they are the ones who matter. Most of the Ethiopians will tell you they like American people but they do not like the foreign policies of your government. You have not seen the Osama bin Laden watches at the market?"

"Bin Laden watches? You've got to be kidding. No, I

haven't seen them. I'm not allowed to go to the market."

"That is a shame," Teddy said, nodding sympathetically. "But I am certain we can find a way around that problem." He grinned at me, and I knew I had made my first friend.

. . .

All of a sudden I remembered I was still lost and alone in the middle of the Ethiopian bush, only now with a goofy smile on my muddy, sweaty face.

Enough daydreaming, Lucy. Nothing has changed! You're still lost and sick, and Psycho Markos is still out here trying to hunt you down. So get moving.

And I did. I followed Moses while the day grew hotter and hotter, eating a fig now and then when I got really hungry and making bush stops when necessary, which was a lot. I couldn't stop thinking about the lions—how they looked, how they made me feel. And just the unbelievable, mind-boggling fact that they had saved my life.

My lion daydreams kept me going for a while, but finally it was too sweltering and I was too tired to keep walking. I needed a nap. I chose a ficus tree because it gave the most shade. Leaning my back against its broad trunk, I fell asleep before I got to *four Mississippi*.

When I woke up, the first thing I noticed was that I felt cool for the first time since—well, since. *As long as I keep my eyes closed, there's a chance it never happened, that this is all a dream.* But I knew it wasn't a dream. Because if I had really been sleeping in my own bed, there wouldn't have been something *crawling up my leg*!

"Ech!!!" I screamed, too freaked out to care if anyone heard me, smacking the big brown spider off my leg and furiously kicking at the same time. I hopped up on my good foot and shook my whole body like some deranged punk dancer, making sure there were no more of them burrowing in my clothes—or under my skin.

Normally I don't mind bugs. In fact, I think bugs are the unsung heroes of our planet. Really. Think about how many insectivores there are, all those millions of creatures who wouldn't be able to exist without bugs to eat. Not to mention all the good things bugs do for humans. Like leeches that help repair veins in damaged skin or maggots that painlessly eat decaying flesh off burn victims. Where would medicine be without them? But that didn't mean I wanted to play host to some hairy arachnid. Gratitude has its limits.

I checked my watch. It was almost three o'clock already—time to get moving. The sky had clouded over, giving me a lot of relief from the heat. Walking would be easier now, I told myself, trying to think positive. *I should be able to put a lot of distance between me and my three murderous abductors before I have to find another tree to sit awake in all night, totally defenseless and completely vulnerable to anyone or anything that might find me there.*

Sometimes it's hard to look on the bright side.

I hobbled alongside Moses for what felt like forever. After I figured out how to tilt my bad foot up and just walk on the heel, it didn't hurt nearly as much. I didn't see any mammals, but the birdlife was fantastic. It was easy to recognize a flock of vulturine guinea fowl by their electric-blue bellies, as vibrant as any peacock's. I didn't see any weavers, but I saw lots of their nests—it's incredible how they can live inside what looks like just a dense ball of twigs and grass. And every so often I'd catch a flash of brilliant color, rollers and bee-eaters darting from tree to tree.

But the birds weren't enough to distract me

completely, and as the sun traveled lower in the sky, worry turned to fear. Salvation wasn't happening today. I was going to have to spend another night in the forest.

Dusk meant it was time to look for a sleeping tree, or at least a hiding-for-the-night tree, since if the night before was anything to go by, I doubted I would do much sleeping. I was getting better at tree selection, and I actually felt pretty proud of myself when it took me only a few minutes to locate the perfect candidate: a medium-size ficus.

Easy to climb? Check. Lots of leaf coverage? Check. No snakes? Check. Comfy branch? Check. Well, sort of.

I went back to Moses, "cleaned" and rewrapped my bandage (miracle of miracles—still no infection), brushed my teeth, and had a long drink. One last bush stop and up I went. There would be no five-minute rest under any umbrella tree tonight.

Which was pretty ironic, because it rained. No, it poured. It deluged. It *monsooned.* Really, I shouldn't have been surprised. This was April. April is usually the start of the rainy season.

And all of a sudden the whole thing struck me as hilarious. I mean the *whole* thing. Wandering around the bush, hanging out with monkeys, getting saved by lions, and now, most of all, hiding all night in a tree, absolutely completely soaking wet. I laughed so hard I almost fell off my branch, the kind of laugh where you can't even breathe anymore but you can't stop, either. I shrieked and cackled and wheezed with laughter, not caring who heard me or what heard me. Not caring about anything at all.

Chapter Nineteen

Day Five

The morning was sunny again, and my fit of insanity seemed to have passed with the rain. I was starving, but my last few figs were a glob of mush in my soggy pockets. I tried to clean my pockets out, without much success. Rainwater had pooled in the tree's long oval leaves, and I tipped leaf after leaf into my mouth until I wasn't thirsty anymore.

Grabbing my walking stick from the foot of the ficus where I'd left it the night before, I headed back to Moses. After months of dry weather, the ground had soaked up all the rainwater and was surprisingly solid, not muddy at all. I was actually happy about my damp clothes, because I figured they'd feel good when the day got really hot again.

I was still walking through trees, but I could see tall grass to the west. Moses was headed north, so I was too. Even though I hadn't found any people or villages yet, following the stream was still the best plan I could come up with.

After an hour or so I needed a five-minute rest. I wasn't sleepy, just bone tired, and I needed to give my muscles a break. So I picked my way around a bunch of small holes in the ground, making my way toward a tree I could lean against.

Just before I reached the tree, the ground collapsed beneath my good foot. I was ankle deep in the earth before I realized I had stumbled into an aardvark burrow. And it took me several more seconds after that to realize a warthog was glaring at me from one of the holes!

I know I said I love warthogs, but I was just talking about how they look. Even though they usually run away from anything they consider threatening, they have been known to kill people—by goring them with their long pointed tusks. I cursed myself for not paying closer attention to the holes. It's not like I didn't know that sounders—that's what groups of warthogs are called—usually live in abandoned aardvark burrows. Just like I also know that warthogs can run really fast, and even with two good feet on my best day there's no way I could outpace one.

But that didn't stop me from screaming my head off like a lunatic and running away—which, by the way, was exactly the wrong thing to do. You're supposed to back away slowly from a dangerous animal, but my flight response kicked in, and I forgot everything I'd ever learned about how to behave in the wild.

I ignored my poor foot and ran as fast as I could, craning my neck around to see if I was being followed. Which is why I slammed right into the two girls who had just appeared out of nowhere and I landed on my back in the dirt.

"*Ya barra!*" said one of the girls, who had fallen on top of me. I had no idea what her words meant.

"Oh my God," I said, staring up in disbelief.

One girl looked about my age, and the other one was probably seven or eight. They wore leather skirts, short in front, long in the back, open at the sides, and decorated with beads and shells in patterns along the edges. Their hairstyle was amazing: hundreds of tiny braids cut short around their faces and coated with some kind of paste or oil that gave their hair a reddish sheen. Equally incredible was their jewelry. They both had on little shell earrings, stacks of narrow gold bracelets around their wrists and silver ones around their elbows and below their knees, plus two necklaces, a long beaded one and a silver metal choker. The younger girl had a whittled toothbrush stick in her mouth, and she carried a plastic water jug strapped to her back with a piece of twine. It was full, so I guessed they were on their way back from getting water.

They stared at me, and I had to give them credit for keeping a straight face. As exotic as they looked to me, what must I, the raggedy mud girl, have looked like to them? Awkwardly, the little one and I struggled to our feet. I pressed my hands together, and bowed. *"Ashama,"* I said, using one of the only Oromo words I know. Hello.

Instantly, they broke into big smiles.

"Gimme pen?" asked the little girl. The older one elbowed her in the ribs. I guess tourism has made its way to the lower Oromo region.

The girls stood close to me and touched my shirt and my arms. It reminded me of being examined by the lions. Had that really been just the day before? But you can bet I recognized salvation when I saw it. Somehow I had to communicate with these kids and get them to help me. I pointed at my chest. "Lucy," I said.

The older girl pointed at me. "Lucy!" she repeated, and then, pointing at herself, "Didessa."

"Didessa" I said, ecstatic. They got it! The younger girl told me her name was Dilla.

"Can you help me?" I asked them. Even though I knew they wouldn't understand the words, I hoped they would get my meaning. But they didn't. They just looked confused.

"Help me," I pleaded. "I need help. Please . . . I'm sick." I pointed to my foot and held my stomach in a desperate pantomime. "I'm lost. I need to find my mother. Mother. *Emama.*" Tears welled in my eyes. I held out my hands, begging them to understand me.

They did. Didessa wrapped her arm around my waist and Dilla grabbed my walking stick and followed us, dragging it behind her.

"*Amasegenallo,*" I whispered, drying my wet cheek on my shoulder. "Thank you."

 183

Chapter Twenty

Their village was only a twenty-minute walk away, but even though my new friends practically carried me there, I didn't know if I would make it. I was so weak from exhaustion and hunger. While we walked (well, they walked, I hobbled), Dilla ran ahead to clear away stones and branches from my path. I was so grateful for their help I kept thanking them over and over in every language I could think of: English, Spanish, French, Italian, German, Arabic, Amharic—every language but theirs, because I didn't know how to say thank you in Oromo. With rescue miraculously, impossibly becoming a reality, I felt more and more anxious. How long would it be until I could call my parents? And how long would it take them to get here? I knew Markos had to be looking for me; there was no way he'd give up, especially since I had made him so angry. I tried to figure out how long the wait would be. There'd be no cell service, so we'd have to go to the nearest real town for a telephone. An airplane ride from Addis couldn't take more than two hours, so it all depended on how far away that real town was and whether someone had a car or even a mule to take us there.

By the time we reached the cluster of small grass huts, we were surrounded by swarms of children who had seen us coming and spread the word to their friends. Most of the boys wore nothing but short skirts that hung down only to about mid-thigh. The skirts were made out of pieces of narrow cloth that they had just wrapped around their waists a couple of times. They all wore their hair very short and shaved in front—so that they were totally bald until halfway across their heads—and then there were ring patterns shaved into what was left of their hair. The boys had on almost as much jewelry as the girls: multiple earrings, wide gold bracelets on both wrists and one elbow, and thin strings of tiny red and blue beads around their necks. A lot of the kids, boys and girls, wore bands around the backs of their heads with two long feathers stuck into the side. Some of the girls also had metal plates sticking out from their headbands like skinny baseball cap visors.

In addition to the jewelry, some of the older kids had decorative scars all over their bodies, tiny lines or dots in columns and rows covering their stomachs, shoulders, and backs. The older boys wore bright face paint, thick bands of red with white polka dots outlining their eyes, noses, and mouths.

Hands reached out to touch my arms, my hair, my clothes. I was *ferenji* again, probably the weirdest-looking *ferenji* they'd ever seen. I felt a tug and looked down to find a toddler holding my shirt, her runny nose dripping all the way to her chin—but, hey, who was I to pass judgment on the way she looked? The kids greeted me with big smiles and asked tons of questions, none of which I could understand. I tried to be friendly, tried to figure out what people were saying, but after everything that had happened over the last four days, I was beginning to think I might actually pass out.

All the commotion had attracted the attention of the grown-ups, some of whom came over to see what the fuss was about. An older woman took one look at me and sent the kids away with a clap and a few short commands. The next thing I knew, the woman was gently guiding me to one of the nearby huts. She talked to me in a soothing voice the whole time, and I understood that there was an international language of motherhood, no translation needed. She saw a sick kid, and she was going to make her better.

The round hut was shaped like a turtle shell. It was so low to the ground that I had to stoop to get inside, and even as small as I am, I could stand fully upright only in the center. The walls were made of a mixture of mud and grass, and the domed roof was entirely thatched grass. In the middle of the packed dirt floor was a cooking area, with a covered dish, a bunch of gourds, two baskets, and some cooking utensils nearby. A few animal skins made up the rest of the contents of the house. Automatically my brain estimated the total area of the space. How many people shared these one hundred square feet? Five? Six? More?

The woman was my size, with fragile-looking bones

like birds' legs. I was surprised by how strong she was: She used those skinny arms to roll out a heavy-looking straw mat, and then she gestured for me to sit down. I thought I would faint with hunger when she opened a clay pot and spooned out something that looked like cream of wheat into a small bowl. She gave it to me, along with fresh milk that she served in a cup made from a cow's horn. It was sweetened with honey that I knew must have come from one of the barrel-shaped straw hives I had seen hanging from the trees outside. The cereal tasted heavenly, and even though I knew I should eat slowly, I couldn't help wolfing it down.

While I was eating, another woman came into the hut, younger and taller than the first. She was using both hands to balance a large black earthenware jug on top of some rags on her head. Carefully, she placed the jug over the cooking fire for a couple of minutes and then poured warm water from the jug into a bowl. What she did next surprised me. She took my face in her hands and studied it, opened my mouth, lifted my eyelids, turned my head right and left. When she moved on to the rest of my body, I realized she was looking me over to see where I might be hurt, and I cried because it felt so good, finally, to be cared for.

The women helped me take off my clothes. It felt weird and a little embarrassing to have people washing me, but soothing at the same time. The whole experience was so unreal, my nakedness was just one more bizarre thing. Together the women washed the mud and filth from my hair and body, scrubbing when necessary and pausing to gently unwrap my wounded foot. When they saw the gash, they frowned and the older woman left the hut, returning a few minutes later with a brownish paste, which she smeared on the cut. It stung like crazy, but I didn't complain.

All this time they spoke to each other quietly, except when they found some fig remains in my pockets, and then they laughed. I sat mute, too worn out to speak. At last, when I was reasonably clean and my foot was bound with a fresh rag, the first woman handed me back my clothes. They were so dirty I hated to put them on again, but it was clear from the very few objects in the hut that these villagers were so poor they had nothing else to give me.

The women knelt in front of me with expectant expressions on their faces. I guessed they wanted me to start, and so, pointing to my chest, I said very slowly and clearly, "Lucy. Hoffman."

"Lucy. Hoffman," they repeated in unison.

"American," I said. "United States of America. U-S-A."

"America." They nodded.

So far, so good. I knew what I wanted to say next. I wanted to tell them my mother was the American ambassador and ask them to please call her right way. But I knew they wouldn't get any of that, so I just said, "*Emama*, Addis Ababa." Then sticking out my left thumb and pinky and holding my hand to my ear in a gesture that I hoped resembled a telephone, I said, "Call her?"

I couldn't tell if they understood or not. The women spoke to each other briefly and then got up and waved at me to follow them outside. After the dim light in the hut, the bright sun was blinding. I shaded my eyes with my hand and squinted at the group of men who approached us. Two of them carried traditional headrests, small wooden stands that I recognized from the museum in Addis. Another had a rifle slung across his shoulder. All together, they were pretty intimidating. I noticed one man was much younger than the rest—a teenager, actually—and he was the one who spoke to me.

"I am Bikila," he said. He was tall for an Ethiopian, close to my dad's height, and his body was decorated with the same scars I had seen on the others. I tried not to stare, but, really, that six-inch skirt of his didn't leave much to the imagination. It's funny: My mother wouldn't let me out of the house in a skirt like that, but here you can't go out without one.

"You speak English?" *Hallelujah!*

"A little. From missionaries. Go slow, please." Bikila smiled, his teeth white and even, and I couldn't help noticing that underneath all that red paint he was really cute.

"Okay," I said. "My name is Lucy Hoffman. I was kidnapped. Do you understand *kidnapped*?" He shook his head.

"Stolen," I explained. "Two men and one woman stole me from my house. They took me away from my mother."

"I understand," said Bikila. "Say more."

"I escaped—ran away. Now I want to go home to

my mother and father." I took a deep breath. "Will you help me go home?"

Bikila turned to the others. I guessed he was translating what I had just told him. While they debated, I tapped my fingers nervously on my walking stick. What would I do if they said no? What could I possibly do? One man in particular seemed to be in charge. He spoke the most and everyone looked to him at the end for a verdict.

Finally, Bikila turned back to me. "We help you go home."

I burst into tears. The men exchanged looks, thinking I don't know what. Probably regretting that they had offered to help the crazy girl. It took a lot of willpower, but I pulled myself together.

"*Amasegenallo.* Thank you," I said, trying to sound sane. "I live in Addis Ababa. My mother is Willa Hoffman. She is the American ambassador to Ethiopia—" That got a reaction. It usually does. "Do you have a telephone? We can call her, and she will come for me."

Bikila shook his head with a sorry expression. "We do not have telephone here. We go to different village.

But . . ." He paused.

"But?" I prompted.

"Today is holiday. We have *ukuli bula*. We go to village after."

Ukuli bula. The leaping over the bulls. I had seen pictures and read about it at the Ethnological Museum in Addis. It's a ceremony that marks the transition to manhood, where young boys have to run across the backs of a whole row of bulls without falling off, after which they're considered men and ready for marriage. I used to dream about being able to see something like this, but not *now,* not this way.

"Please, Bikila, please can we go now?" I begged.

He shook his head. "Abba say no," he said firmly. *Abba* means "father" in Oromo, and it can also be used as a term of respect. I guessed he was talking about the older man who seemed to be in charge. "We go after. We go tonight."

Tonight. That left hours for Markos to find me. And when he did, armed with his rifle and a pack of lies, what would these villagers do? Would they believe the African man or the American girl?

 193

Chapter Twenty-One

For the next two hours the whole village was busy getting ready. More jewelry, more face paint, more feathers. Some of the older girls covered their entire bodies in the same red stuff they used in their hair. I realized that the pictures I had seen of tribal people had in no way prepared me for the real thing. In books, tribal people look so *weird*. I could never understand why people would want to carve scars on their bodies or put plates in their lips or cover their hair with paste. But in person—well, is it really so different from all the piercings people have at home and all the makeup they wear?

Being a *ferenji* didn't get me off the hook. I was

lying exhausted on the dusty ground next to the hut where the women had bathed and fed me when a group of girls led me away to join them under a shady tree. Before I knew it, two of them were arranging my hair in rows of tiny braids like theirs and coating my head—not to mention my face, arms, and legs—with the red paste. "No, really," I said. "It's okay. You don't have to do that." But they just laughed and kept braiding. *If Tana and Teddy could only see me now.*

When the chanting started, I knew the ceremony was about to begin. Everyone gathered in an open field, where a dozen men were holding eight emaciated bulls together in a straight line. The bulls were snorting and pawing the ground while the men held them by their long, curved horns to keep them steady. All the girls were yelling like crazy. I stood with Bikila and the two women who had helped me. At first Bikila tried to explain what was going on, but everyone around us was so loud he gave up.

When the crowd parted to let the boys through, I gasped. They were stark naked! Well, except for these skinny little strings they wore crossed over their shoulders, but those didn't count. I tried hard not to stare, but how could I help it?

The first boy stepped forward, and the crowd chanted louder. He looked around nervously before setting his shoulders, taking a deep breath, and making a running jump for the bull on the end nearest him. He made it up onto the bull's back and started stumbling down the line, holding his arms out wide for balance. It had to have been incredibly hard, because aside from the fact that the animals were struggling to get away, Ethiopian cattle have huge humps on their backs, so the boy's path was both unsteady and uneven.

The boy made it to the third bull before falling, and it took him two more tries to get all the way across. But when he did, the crowd let out a gigantic cheer, and there was dancing and singing as if we were at a high school pep rally.

The fourth boy was taking his turn and I was wondering how much longer I'd be able to keep standing. That's when I saw them.

Markos, Dawit, and Helena.

I grabbed Bikila's arm and yelled into his ear, "That's them! That's them!" He read the terror in my face and shoved me behind him, shielding me from view. My whole body trembled. I crouched down low, so close to Bikila that I could follow the trickle of sweat running down his dark brown skin, bumping over the neat rows of scars on his back.

The chanting died out as more people noticed the intruders. Peering through the space between Bikila's arm and his body, I had a clear view of Markos. He slapped his hand against his gun while he talked, just to make sure any idiot could tell he meant business. I kept seeing the black dog lying dead in the dirt.

Now Abba was talking to them. I couldn't understand a word, of course, but I could guess. Markos was probably making up some ridiculous story about what a liar I am and how my parents sent him to get me, how worried they were about me, blah, blah, blah. For all I knew, he might even have been telling them Helena is my mother. Who were they going to believe?

I leaned my head out another inch for a better view, and in the same second Dawit turned in my direction. I froze like a wild animal caught in a spotlight. *Maybe if I don't move, I'll be invisible.* But, no, Dawit's eyes found mine. It was so quick I couldn't be 100 percent positive he had seen me, but I was pretty sure he had. At least it felt like he had. But then he turned around again as though nothing had happened.

I was stunned. Was it actually possible that Dawit would let me escape? *"I am sorry, Lucy,"* he had said. Maybe he really was.

Now it looked like Markos was getting angry. He started yelling and jabbing the air with his finger. I saw Abba shake his head, and then Markos ran to the nearest hut and leaned inside. Two of the village men ran after him and tried to pull him out. With all the fighting going on, no one noticed when Abba caught Bikila's eye. Bikila nodded and the older man gave a small thrust of his chin.

"Go!" Bikila whispered to me. "We go now." Waves of relief flooded over me as we melted back into the crowd and hurried to squat down behind the nearest hut. I couldn't believe it—the villagers were letting me go!

"Bikila, what happened?" I asked as soon as we were hidden.

"He say you run away and your father ask him to find you."

 198

"But why did Abba tell you to hide me?"

Bikila's face grew serious. "That man is very bad. He has angry *zar*."

I knew from the Ethnological Museum that a *zar* is a person's inner spirit. So Markos has an angry *zar*. I guess that's one way of looking at it.

"He has no respect. He yell to Abba. He want to go inside house after Abba say no." Bikila stood up. "We go now, Lucy."

I nodded, but a wild hope made me hesitate. I grabbed Bikila's arm. "Bikila, wait a sec—"

He stopped.

"Are we anywhere near Guge?"

A huge grin lit up Bikila's face, the circles of red and white paint crinkling around his eyes. "Foosball!"

Teddy.

Chapter Twenty-Two

We sat on the floor of the *tukul,* Teddy, his little sister, his father, and I, watching his mother perform the coffee ceremony. Teddy's house looked different from the ones in the tribal village. It was round, with walls made of mud and grass, but it had a pointed roof, and it was wider in diameter and a lot taller. You could stand up anywhere inside. People here dressed differently too. Some, like Teddy, his father, and his sister, had on Western clothes, and others, like his mother, wore national clothes.

Bikila and I had walked for about two miles. It took us an hour, first through some woods and then along a dirt road, although it probably would have taken about half the time if I hadn't been in such lousy shape. It drove me crazy to go so slowly. I kept waiting for Markos to spring out from behind the next tree, rifle cocked and ready. Even now I couldn't fully relax. I remembered how furious he had been back in the tribal village. *He must be out of his mind by now.*

Bikila had gone back to his village for the big party after the *ukuli bula.* I cried when he left, and he gave me one of his hair feathers as a keepsake, which I now wore in my own braided, red, oiled hair, completing my look as a tribal Pippi Longstocking.

Teddy's mother spread lavender branches and eucalyptus leaves over the dirt floor, filled a metal pan with pale green fresh coffee beans, and placed the pan over the cooking fire. The smell of the roasting beans mixed with the scent of eucalyptus and lavender was clean and potent. While we waited for the coffee, Teddy and I shared a dish of popcorn, some half popped, some burned, all of it nutty and delicious. The walls of the *tukul* curved in and down to make two narrow sleeping platforms, and I sat with my back against one of them.

I was thinking that Teddy seemed different here in

his own home, bigger and older somehow, and I must have had a strange look on my face because he asked, "What is it?"

"I don't know. I was just thinking that you look different."

"Really?" he said, tugging on one of my pasty braids and smiling his gorgeous smile. "You do not look different at all."

Teddy's mother offered me a turn grinding the beans with a mortar and pestle. I was glad to have something helpful to do because there was no way I could even begin to talk about what had happened. It had been all I could do just to get myself to say the word *kidnapped* and ask them to call my mother.

When the coffee was ready, Teddy's mother added one part sugar for every two parts liquid and passed around the cups, smiling and nodding when she gave me mine. It tasted almost like tea, with none of the bitterness coffee usually has. Teddy's family seemed to sense my need for quiet, and we drank our coffee in silence. Conversation would have been difficult anyway, since Teddy's family doesn't speak English.

When we were done, Teddy asked me if I wanted

to go outside for a while. I was grateful for something to distract me from counting the minutes until my parents arrived. Teddy pointed out the main sites of the village as we walked. "That is the house of Yonas, my laziest friend," he said. "And there is the papaya tree I fell from when I was six years old and broke my arm."

Some boys were playing soccer in the road, using a bundle of rags for a ball. Teddy waved at them, and they stopped their game to stare at me. I noticed several women wearing traditional long skirts and white *netala* shawls and using pink plastic umbrellas as sunshades. Skinny sheep with long fluffy tails dozed by the roadside, and humpback cows were grazing in the fields around us, though I couldn't imagine what they could find to eat in the bare, dusty earth.

We had almost reached the end of the village when I spotted it, standing in all its glory surrounded by teams of worshipping teenage boys.

"Behold!" Teddy said, grinning. "The famous Guge foosball table."

"A beacon for lost American teenagers," I added, pointing at it with my walking stick.

"Lucy . . ." Teddy wasn't smiling anymore.

"Yeah?"

"You could have been lost forever."

"I know," I said softly.

Teddy turned to me and took my free hand in both of his. Then he leaned down and gently pressed his forehead against mine. "I am happy that you are safe," he whispered.

It wasn't my first kiss, but by Ethiopian standards it was close enough.

Chapter Twenty-Three

We heard the helicopters way before we saw them—that unmistakable *chop-chop-chop* sound that signaled the real, true end of my ordeal. In seconds, three Black Hawks had landed in the field, and soldiers in black body armor poured out the open sides. Villagers scattered toward their huts, their hands over their faces to protect them from the swirling dust.

But I barely noticed any of it because there they were at last, my mother and father, stooping low under the propellers and gazing around wildly. All I wanted to do was run to them, but for some reason I couldn't move.

"Lucy!" Mom screamed, and the sound of her

voice freed me. I let go of Teddy and started limping toward them as fast as I could—and then tripped over a rock and fell flat on my face. I struggled to get up, but I didn't have to because all of sudden Mom and Dad were there. They pulled me into their arms and the three of us clung together, crying. Mom was practically hysterical, and Dad just kept smoothing my hair back from my face and saying my name over and over again. "Lucy, my Lulu."

And all I could say was, "I'm sorry. I'm so sorry. I'm sorry."

• • •

Flying back to Addis in the helicopter, Mom told me how awful she felt about everything that had happened, that it was all her fault and we would move back to the States immediately. "Our house is so close to the high school you can walk there yourself. No more drivers, no guards. You can be like every other kid."

I looked down at the rocky fields and terraced hills, the grazing cattle, and the flock of Abyssinian rollers soaring over it all.

"No way," I said.

"Lu?" Dad asked.

I pressed my face against the window. I could still see Teddy and his family waving good-bye. They would stay there, I was sure, until we were just a speck on the horizon.

"How can I leave?" I asked, tracing an invisible pattern on the glass. "I haven't had a chance to really live here yet."

"But, sweetheart, don't you want to go home, where you can be with people like yourself? After everything that's happened, how can you still want to live here?"

I turned to him. "But I *am* with people like myself, Daddy. You and Mom, Iskinder, Tana and Teddy, Bikila . . ."

My parents exchanged looks. "You're tired, Lucy. We'll talk about this later."

"Yeah, I'm tired, but you don't get it. Bikila and the rest of the people in his village, they protected me from Markos. They didn't care that he was African and I'm American or that he's an adult and I'm a kid. None of that stuff mattered because they knew I was telling the truth."

"How do you think they knew Markos was the one

who was lying?" asked Mom, sounding genuinely curious.

I smiled faintly. "They said they could tell he had an angry *zar*."

"Of course," Dad said, with not a little sarcasm. "An angry *zar*. What else could it have been?"

"Oh, lay off, Dan. Given everything that's happened, an angry *zar* is as reasonable a justification as we're likely to find."

I stared at my mother, my newfound ally, totally shocked—and almost choked when she actually winked at me.

Coming home was when I really lost it. As soon as I saw Iskinder, I basically collapsed on him, crying hysterically until I had turned his jacket into a red pasty mess.

"Iskinder," I said when I could talk again, "can you ever forgive me for being so unbelievably horrendous to you?"

"All that matters to me, Lucy, is that you are safe."

I thought of something else. "What about my mom?" I whispered. "Was she mad at you for leaving me at Tana's? Because I'll tell her it was all my fault—which it totally was," I added.

"There is no need for that, Lucy. Your mother knows you very well."

We both had a laugh at that, and then it was time for me to see the doctor, who was waiting for me at the residence. He gave me medicine for my stomach but said there was nothing more he needed to do for my foot. It was too late for stitches, and the herb mixture that the women had used had disinfected the wound.

Finally, I went to my room. Nothing I had imagined came close to what I saw in the mirror over my dresser. My skin, my hair, the filthy clothes. I was a mess. I gently extracted Bikila's feather from my hair and laid it on top of my dresser. Later I'd figure out someplace special to keep it, but for now I wanted it out where I could see it all the time. One by one, I untangled the braids, and my hair frizzed out like one of those cartoon characters with her finger in an electric socket. Then I peeled off my clothes and threw them straight into the wastebasket.

After the longest shower of my life, I put on my

bathrobe and looked in the mirror again, leaning forward until I was only three inches from the glass. I carefully examined my face and eyes. It seemed so weird: After everything that I had been through, how could it not *show*? How could there be no visible sign of the person I had become?

There was a knock on my door, and I heard Tana say, "Lucy?"

I thought I had cried myself out with Iskinder, but I was wrong. We sank down on the floor together, hugging and sobbing until I said, "Wow, imagine if I had actually died."

Tana laughed. "Oh, I have. Lucy, we never should have gone out. This was all my fault."

"You're kidding, right?" I said to her. "First of all it was my brilliant idea, and second of all, if we hadn't sneaked out that day, those guys would have just found another time to do it. Please don't blame yourself, Tana. It really wasn't your fault at all."

"I cannot help it. How do you know they would have found another opportunity?"

"Because I'm the idiot who kept sneaking out all the time. Face it, I made it easy for them. Hey," I said, changing the subject, "guess what? I went to an *ukuli bula* ceremony—and the boys were *naked*!"

"Really?! What did they look like?"

I moved up to my bed and patted the spot next to me. "Come here. I'll tell you everything."

Epilogue

One Month Later

I had it wrong, of course.

The kidnapping had nothing to do with Mom's committee, although it did have to do with drug dealers. There was this big-deal Pakistani drug lord, Syed Ibrahim Kausri, who was on America's most-wanted list for exporting heroin to the United States. Markos and Dawit worked for him, transporting drugs from Ethiopia to Kenya. And—get this—Helena was a flight attendant for British Airways who earned money on the side by smuggling heroin on her flights from Africa to the States. The police had captured Kausri in Ethiopia and were going to send him to the U.S. to be tried and locked up there for the rest of his life. Kausri's plan was a kind of prisoner exchange—let him go, or else it would be his life for mine. Lucky for me it didn't work out that way.

It took a while for the excitement to die down. For a few weeks I was famous. Newspapers all over the world ran front-page stories about me; TV shows wanted to interview me (guess what my mother had to say about that?). Everyone wanted to hear more about *The Abduction of the Ambassador's Daughter!!* and *Girl Saved by Wild Lions!!* And naturally everyone had an opinion. Some of the wildlife experts said that my crying must have sounded like a cub mewing and made the lions protective. Others said the lions were going to eat me and just hadn't gotten around to it yet. Personally, I have no idea why the lions did what they did. But I know I felt a connection to them, and it was more than just gratitude for saving my life. I wonder if the lions felt connected to me too.

Mom and I are getting along much better now. A couple of days after it was all over, I asked her what she did when she found out I was gone.

"I cried," she said.

I was stunned. Mom crying? "But what about

calling the police and the army and the president and giving them all hell and telling them they'd better find your daughter in five seconds or heads would roll?"

She smiled. "Oh, I did all of that first. But then I sent them away to do their jobs, and I closed the door to my office, sat down on the floor, and cried.

"Lucy," she went on, "you're my . . . I could never . . ." Her voice broke, and she looked at me with tears in her eyes.

"It's okay, Mom. Everything turned out all right, didn't it?"

Actually, it turned out better than all right. We're staying. All of us together, as a family. Dad took a job teaching economics at Addis Ababa University, and Mom tries to be home for dinner at least three nights a week, which she does—well, most of the time. Not only is my curfew lifted, but Mom and Dad promised to take me on trips to see every last inch of this country before it's time to move on to the next one. Tana and Teddy are coming with us to the Simien Mountains as soon as school is out in June. I'll finally get to see the gelada baboons!

Tana is officially going to London next fall, and

I'm trying not to think about life here without her. At least she'll be back for Christmas and summer vacation, and she promises she'll come with us on some of our adventures. Of course Teddy will still be here—and that's turning out to be a whole new kind of adventure.

Speaking of adventure, I've upped my game drives to twice a week. The first time I returned to the bush it felt like a homecoming. Dahnie drove over the familiar trails, and I stared out the open windows at the tall grass, imagining a flash of gold fur, wisps of a black mane, the glint of an amber eye. Watching me. Waiting.

Author's Note

Escape Under the Forever Sky was inspired by a true story. In June 2005, a twelve-year-old girl was kidnapped from her village in southwestern Ethiopia and held captive for a week before she managed to escape. Running through the forest, the girl happened upon three wild lions. The lions surrounded her and chased off her abductors, standing guard for several hours until the police arrived.

Two things drew me to this story the instant I read it. The first was the image of a girl alone in a forest, surrounded by wild lions. What did that feel like? I wondered. What was she thinking? She was never named in any of the news articles, so I had to find a way to answer those questions myself.

I started by doing a lot of research, interviewing experts, and traveling to Ethiopia. While the people and the events in the book are fictional, almost all the descriptive details are factual (yes, Selassie did employ a pillow bearer, a keeper of the cloth, and a minister of the pen).

The second thing that drew me to this story was the idea of bridging the differences to make connections with beings unlike ourselves. Witness the account of the lioness in Kenya that adopted a baby antelope, guarding it fiercely for weeks. Or the hundred-year-old tortoise that acted like a father to a baby hippo that had been orphaned by a tsunami.

Lucy is an American girl in an African country, a child among adults; she is white, and almost everyone around her is black. And yet the people in the tribal village see past all of those differences. They recognize that Lucy is telling the truth and offer her the help she so desperately needs. As the curator at the National Museum in Addis says to Lucy, and as a curator at the National Museum in Addis said to me when I visited Ethiopia, "Nationality and religion are just politics. We are all one species."

Acknowledgments

Nick, Joe, and Maya, eleven days were just the tip of the iceberg. Thank you for being the best cheering squad, the most faithful readers, and the all-around greatest family ever. I promise the next time I need to travel across the planet to research a book, we'll all go together. And thank you to the rest of my family, especially Mom, Dad, Jen, Ron, Jake, and Leni, for all your support.

Thank you, Eileen Katz, Sam Hoffman, Patty Saidenberg, Greg Dalvito, Lynn Goldner, and Tali Balas, and Rebecca Davis, for your advice and encouragement.

Ahmed Beshir and Daniel Shewalem, thank you for introducing me to your extraordinary country, and for patiently fielding about ten thousand questions. Thanks to Luke Hunter of the Wildlife Conservation Society, without whom I never would have known what a lion feels like.

Special thanks to my agent, Judy Heiblum, my editor, Victoria Rock, and the rest of the team at Chronicle Books.

Finally, to my first reader, alter ego, and cherished friend, Marc Acito, who urged me to climb the mountain—and then held my hand all the way up—*amasegenallo*.

Reader's Guide

- **What are some of the ways in which living in Ethiopia is different from living in your country? What are some of the similarities?**

- In the beginning of the novel, Lucy believes her mother cares more about her career than she does about her daughter. **Do you think that is true? What about Lucy's father and his career?**

- Lucy feels free to "just be herself" when she is in the bush. **Is there a place that makes you feel that way?**

- In Chapter Five, Tana describes what it's like being a girl in Ethiopia: "Lucy, if you think it is bad to be a girl here, just imagine what it is like to be a woman. Men are in charge of everything. . . . When I grow up, they will all expect me to behave a certain way just because that is how it has always been. I hate it." **How does that compare to how girls are treated in your country?**

- In Chapter Six, Lucy blames her mother for what happened in the market. Her mother blames her. **Who do you think is right?**

- **Why do you think the lions surrounded Lucy?**

- **Did you expect Abba and the rest of the villagers to believe Markos or Lucy? Why?**

- In Chapter Nine, the curator of the National Museum says to Lucy, "Nationality and religion are just politics. We are all one species." **What do you think he means by that? Do you agree?**